The Two Seeds

❧❧❧ Two Seeds ❧❧❧

Carlton Page

authorHOUSE®

AuthorHouse™
1663 Liberty Drive
Bloomington, IN 47403
www.authorhouse.com
Phone: 1-800-839-8640

Published by AuthorHouse   12/01/2014

ISBN: 978-1-4969-5582-1 (sc)
ISBN: 978-1-4969-5583-8 (e)

❧✿❧ Chapter 1 ❧✿❧

Awakening on the top of a skyscraper, X was questioning his existence at this very point in time. "Why am I still here?" He looked at his hand for any signs of broken bones, cuts, or even scrapes. Nothing seemed to be there, then a voice suddenly was heard from his blind spot.

"I'm sure you have many questions. I can answer one. Yes, you are dead, but I am here to give you the chance to use your rebirth for a great and mighty cause."

X was not afraid of this person, however, the fact that they were both standing atop of this building still yearned for questions. "Ok... why are we here and who are you?"

The mysterious man walked up to X, shook his hand and took a bow. "I am Gabri...call me G." X demanded to know why they were there. G then took a couple steps toward the ledge of the skyscraper.

"If we are already dead, what good will that do?"

G then fell backwards off the building, headed toward the ground with bullet-like speed. X ran over to the ledge; as soon as he looked over, G was there, ascending at the same speed he had been falling, landing right beside X. X was excited and at the same time in awe.

"So what you're going to tell me is that I can do that too?" said X.

"You can, but let me ask you something. Do you have faith?"

X thought about this for a second then said, "Well, let's find out." As stepping onto the ledge of the building, he closed his eyes and fell forward.

While descending, it was not as fast a free fall as G's, but his mind was caught in a state of deep thought. X thought to himself, What do I believe? As a child, I was always taught that God and Jesus existed in all of us, spiritually and mentally, but no one knows truth. After centuries, no one can prove anything. Then again, why am I free falling in a conscious state of mind? Something must be real, and if it is, I'd like to find out.

As he thought this, G's voice was heard also inside of his mind. "It's real X, and you're about to find out better than any other being in the universe how real it is. And how real things are about to get."

Suddenly, X opened his eyes, mere seconds from his body hitting the pavement. With a burst of energy, a blue aura appears around his body, along with what appeared to be wings made of pure energy. The energy thrust him back toward the top of the skyscraper with lightning speed. G was the one in awe this time, as X landed with a mighty force next to him with the power still pouring out of his eyes.

Looking up at G he said, "Looks like you have a lot to explain."

ꝥ⳽e⳽ꝥ Chapter 2 ꝥ⳽e⳽ꝥ

In a suburban neighborhood, there is a crime scene with several murder weapons. An axe has been firmly planted into the skull of a woman who lays face down in a pool of her own blood, her other limbs of tossed about the room. The second weapon, a Smith and Wesson .500, held with a death grip by the murderer. In one arm lays the corpse of his five-year-old daughter, a huge gaping hole out in the side of her head. It just so turns out that her and daddy have matching holes, except for one detail – daddy is alive.

With slow animation, the body turns its head and opens its eyes, looking around the room in disbelief. "What am I doing back in this shit hole?" Looking at the revolver and then his daughter, he kisses the revolver and drops the body without remorse.

Slowly coming to his feet, he notices a mirror and walks over to check out the damage. Half his face is blown to bits. As he is inspecting his body, he begins to talk to himself. "I could have sworn I took my life minutes ago. I mean dead wife on the floor, check. Stupid annoying brat to my right, check. So what's not adding up?"

As he began to go on, his reflection answered him back. "You're obviously back here for a reason. Your hate fuels you. Look at this carnage; you were made to destroy." At that very second, his reflection peeled itself out of the mirror and changed form, slithering into the shadows.

With the Smith and Wesson pointed into the shadows, he says, "What are you?"

The shadow creature pointed at him. "You and I are the same dead lost souls. All we know is pain and how to deliver it. I am nothing, but a messenger to make sure that you have awakened. That body that holds the key to so much destruction."

With a puzzled look on his face, he replies, "What the fuck are you talking about? You know what? Screw it! I'm going to have a drink." He fires the weapon into the shadows.

The creature slithers underneath his arm, reaching up and grabbing the revolver with immense strength, tossing his body into a bookcase like a rag doll. Wrapping around his leg, swinging and smashing him through a glass table, the creature speaks. "I knew you weren't worthy of that body's potential. I am going to rip your worthless soul right out of your body." The fingertips of the shadow hand turned into leech-like creatures with blood dripping from each tip.

As the body of the murderer lay over the glass from the shattered table, he began to think, Why am I still here and why am I being attacked by an asshole shadow? If my hate fuels me, then I'm about to take this motherfucker out?

The leech hand of the shadow creature was placed upon the murderer's chest. He began to feed on the body's aura. "Yes, I feel the hate and the rage fuel me so that I can become…" and at that very moment he noticed the energy was flowing more rapidly than he expected; it was taking in too much too a point where it began to hurt the creature.

The murderer grabbed the creature's wrist.

"It's a damn shame the very last thing you will hear is the question 'Why,' as in 'Why the fuck is there a hand with leeches sucking something of my chest?'"

The murderer snaps the wrist with little effort and begins to pull back in the stolen aura. "You just fucked with the wrong dead guy today," he said, as the aura flowed back inside of his body.

The creature looked down at its own hand as he too began to realize that it, too, was being drawn into the body. The creature shrieked, "How and why?"

"I kinda like it, Y! That's what you shall call me from now on." The shadow creature was trapped from behind his eyes. "You shall tell me everything I want to know about this power, and you're absolutely right, I do love to destroy but there will never be an answer to the question 'Why?'"

ϾϾϾ Chapter 3 ϾϾϾ

As the the shadow creature was now trapped behind Y's eyes, Y demanded to know the creature's name, the creature spoke, "I am the demon known as Squylir; I am merely a scout for he who reaps and collects souls."

"Ok Squylir, now tell me more about these powers you were trying to steal from me."

Squylir and G began to tell the tale of the great beginning. Millions of years ago, God was lonely in his solitude, and the legend of his power tells that He can create anything at his very command or train of thought, so of his power He created two entities that would bring him amusement – one entity of his good nature the other of more of his impure thoughts. Being that the two entities were made of pure energy, when the two entities collided with one another, it set off a massive chain reaction resulting in an explosion, which n resulted in what appeared to be millions of other smaller life forms and planets thus creating the solar system and the universe itself. The two entities survived the blast, but God knew that keeping them separate would ultimately be better for the survival of the universe they just created and all the life forms that spawned from the explosion. Condensing the power of the entities, God would place the two entities into the different life forms they created to keep them separate from one another so their power would lie dormant for millions of years. Upon creating so many life forms, heaven and hell were created to police the souls of the life forms it has always been said that the souls of the truly divine go to heaven and the souls of the wicked go to hell. Tensions rose between the two realms, as both monitored the earth realm closely and took notice of the bodies that sheltered the entities. Word spread, mostly through the assistants of the Reaper – or the angel of death, who did not take sides in the feud between the opposing sides but just collected the souls because they also fueled his power and payment to travel in between all three worlds. It was not his job to protect the entities, only to guide them into their next vessels. The two assistants to keep track of the entities; one scout was the demon Squylir and the other was the angel Gabriel.

Both Gabriel and Squylir would go against God's wish to keep them apart thinking that if they could awaken the powers they possessed, they could use it to help their team control earth. There would for sure be a winner in the conflict, with Gabriel, of course, wanting to see good prevail and Squylir wanting to see evil conquer.

❧ℭ✺ℭ❧ Chapter 4 ❧ℭ✺ℭ❧

After G explained the legend to X, the latter asked, "What all can I do power-wise?"

G said, "It looks as if you can imagine whatever you want into existence. Try it."

X closed his eyes and began to think of something. When he opened his eyes, a white horse was standing in front of him.

"Oh, a horse is that the best you can do?" G said.

Y closed his eyes and before him was a military-issue tank. "I could have some fun with this, but…" He closed his eyes once more. When he opened them, he was on earth sitting in an 1997 Toyota Supra RZ. "Ok this is nice but…" Snapping his fingers, the car transformed into a highly-modified machine. He flipped a switch to engage the ignition, and the beast roared. Immediately doing a fat burn out, he pulled up to the stop light, and as the tire smoke was clearing he looked to his left a highly modified Subaru wrX STI Impreza 22B sat next to the Supra. At the light, Y revved the beast once more, giving the driver of the 22B the signal that he wanted the challenge. The 22B roared as well. The drivers revved their engines waiting for the light to change, then the light flashed green, and the two cars took off into first gear then second. The Subaru's driver missed third gear while dodging a car. Laughing, Y shifted into fourth gear while almost hitting a bus. The Subaru caught up both cars shifting into fifth gear coming into a steep corner the drivers braked then downshifting the Supra driver kicked the clutch sliding the car around apex of the corner the Subaru downshifted but powered through the corner. Coming to the next corner, the Supra kicked the clutch once more drifting smoothly through it.

Y was overjoyed with this challenger but looking into his rear view mirror noticed that the Subaru also was drifting the corners. Scratching his head. He decided to ditch the Subaru driver through traffic on the next street. He thought he was successful, but as he passed an alley, the Subaru passed in front of him cutting from the alley. Proceeding through a busy street, the Subaru lost the tail of the Supra. Sitting at a red light, Y scratched his head once more then said, "If I see that car again, "ll just blow it up."

❧❦❧ Chapter 5 ❧❦❧

After the race was over, Y sat in the Supra thinking about his next move. "Squylir, if I am the true root of all evil, what does that make the devil?"

"The devil is a fallen angel who started a revolution in hell of misfit souls."

Y pondered for a moment. "So the ideal thing for me to do would be to go to hell and start my own revolution, correct?"

Squylir said nothing.

"Well?"

"Even with the power that lies inside of you, you are not immortal. It would be wise to develop your powers even further before pursuing that position–"

"What do you mean not immortal? Aren't I already dead?"

"This is correct, you are dead, but since you possess the power inside of you, and it has awakened that is the only thing keeping the body animated, although if the body is no more the entity must leave the body, which is why I came to you in the first place, to see to it that the entity find a new home, but since it has awakened inside of you there will be no transportation of the entity into a new body until that body has been destroyed."

Y smiled. "Sounds like a bunch of bullshit to me. So how do we go about training?"

"Seeing as how you have plans to take over hell, the devil has ears everywhere and I'm sure he's already aware of your plans, which means..."

The ground began to tremble underneath Y's feet then suddenly began to split, sending his body hurtling down a huge gaping crack.

As Y fell into the darkness, feeling as if he had been falling forever, he felt a pull at his leg, as if it were dragging him through a tunnel. The dragging was interrupted by a sudden *thud* on a hard surface.

Y could not see a single thing around him he closed his eyes. Snapping his fingers and then opening his eyes revealed a giant cavern lit with hundreds of torches. Y thought to himself, "Damn that was kinda cool," and as he was in mid thought he heard movement from above the cavern wall.

"Show yourself," Y demanded.

A voice echoed back, "Be careful what you wish for."

Looking around for the next sign of movement, Y yelled, "If you're going to attack, do it all ready or don't waste my ti–"

Y's speech was interrupted by the sharp end of a spear almost cutting him in the face. Barely recovering from dodging that attack, another swing of the spear followed. Y also dodged that attack, but he was eager to meet his attacker. Snapping his fingers he met the next spear attack with a halberd of his own and finally saw the winged creature trying to kill him.

The demon stood just a bit taller than he did, with huge wings, the legs of a goat, the upper body of a human and ram's horns, a necklace of skulls and other metals around its neck. His spear was double-sided for swift sweeps and jabs.

Y was not intimidated but knew he better tread cautiously. H jumped back with the halberd, and the demon also jumped back, his massive wings flapping. As he landed, Y launched his attack, thrusting the halberd at the demon The demon dodged his attack and took a swift swing with his own spear. Y dodged by ducking one swing then jumping over the next. The demon spit a fireball from its mouth, engulfing Y in flames. As Y felt the burn, he snapped his fingers, turning his body into ice. The demon flew toward the icicle that was Y, hoping to smash him into pieces. He flung a spear first into Y, but the head of the spear snapped.

The demon's expression on his face was confused. "But how?"

Y's ice body melted, revealing another coat of steel then turned back to normal and struck with the halberd to the chest of the demon, leaving a huge wound.

The demon put his hand to his wound. "Even if you defeat me, many more will come to defend the throne of the Dark King."

Y laughed because he remembered that it was a joke at first, then said with a straight face, "Then it looks like you will be the first of many to fall protecting what's going to be mine." Y's eyes began to glow, as if he were possessed.

The entity was feeding his body with energy, healing his burns. The halberd was now infused with the energy and morphed its shape. Y charged at the demon then disappeared.

The demon was in fear. "Where did you go?"

The torches around them went out suddenly, and the only illuminated object in the room was the morphed halberd. As the demon looked down at it sticking through the middle of its torso, his body then instantly burst into a million pieces. The halberd's light went out there was complete silence.

❧❧❧ Chapter 6 ❧❧❧

After the race was over, X asked G what their next move was.

"We must visit the council of angels for you to receive more training and also take charge of the angel army, although I fear it may not be as easy as you think."

"Was it supposed to be easy nothing is ever that easy? Wait – so why is it going to be difficult?"

"Angels can be quite judgmental."

X was not surprised. "Ok…so how do we get to heaven?"

"Hmmm, good question. How about this – you create the gateway there, and I will open the gates."

"Seriously, you want me to create some portal to a place I have never been?"

"Just do it."

X closed his eyes and began to think. When he opened his eyes, an elevator was in front of him. He and G walked into it.

As the doors closed, G said, "An elevator, huh? How cliché."

X replied, "Shut up."

The elevator began to rise at great speeds until it vanished into time and space and eventually faded into a flash of light. The doors opened at the sound of a *ding*, and the two gentlemen stepped out.

"Way to take the long way, sport," G said.

X looked at him confused, then G pointed to a pair of massive gates. "Why are the gates to heaven so big?" X said.

"Technically, you created the gateway, so this is your own interpretation of the gates of heaven. Again, a cliché."

G walked up to the gates placing his hand upon the massive bar of the gate. It began to open, and heaven was revealed for the first time to the eyes of X. He was stunned because heaven surprisingly looked like another earth except everything was ultra clean and the space was unlimited, but in the middle of the massive space was a large building made entirely of white gold and an assortment of other rare and precious stones and materials.

G pointed to the building. "That's where we go to talk to the council of angels."

X and G made their way to the capitol where they were met at the doors by security. G told X to step back and let him handle it.

X did as he was told. He couldn't hear everything G was saying to the guards, was just waiting for the signal, then finally they were let through.

"What took so long?" X asked G.

"I might be in some trouble."

"Why?"

"For bringing you here."

X shook his head. "Let's just get this over with."

They walked into a conference room filled with what looked like regular men and women One of them spoke. "Why do you bring this man before us today, Gabriel?"

G replied, "Ladies and gentlemen of the council, this is no regular man like me and you. He is an angel – don't you see his wings?"

The council looked over X's body inspecting him from head to toe.

Another council member spoke. "He does appear to have wings, but they do not look like ours so what is he?"

G replied, "This is our trump card, ladies and gentlemen. With him, we can win the battle for our kingdom. He has a special power, and I have seen it for myself."

Another council member spoke. "Care to demonstrate?"

X stepped forward and closed his eyes, and when he opened them a rare extinct animal called the dodo stood before him.

G smacked his forehead. "Ok, look, he has the power to create anything he wants."

Another council member spoke. "A dodo? Not very impressive. We have many of those already here; it's like heaven's pigeon. Such a stupid Bird. But out of curiosity, where does his power come from?"

"His power spawns from the father, much like all of our own," G said. "Now with no further questions, might I ask that we have

13

permission to assimilate the army and make the first strike at the demons?"

The council began to chat among themselves then its leader responded, "Gabriel, you are not even warrior class; you are just the assistant to the reaper. However, we still grant you permission to speak to Michael about the matter, but as for the request to control the army, he must prove to Michael that he is worthy. Seeing as how Michael is the general, we will see how this pans out. This meeting is adjourned."

ϸϾϿϸ Chapter 7 ϸϾϿϸ

The meeting with the council of angels was a bust, still G decided to take X to see Michael. X and G flew over to the military base. X was surprised to see an actual military base in Heaven.

"So who is this Michael guy – is he cool?"

G stopped in mid-flight. "Michael is the archangel, probably the most powerful angel in heaven. Is he cool? Yeah, something like that."

They landed in front of the barracks and were met by more angel guards. One of the guards spoke, "Trespassing on the base is strictly prohibited."

G responded, "We are here to meet with Michael."

The guards drew their swords. "Last chance to leave here unharmed," one said.

X was not impressed. "Or what? Bring it."

G interrupted. "Look, we just want to talk to Michael…orders from the council."

A loud flapping was heard from behind the commotion, and a voice was heard from the back of the guards. 'Stand down. Let me hear what he has to say."

The archangel had arrived. Muscular and tall in stature, he wore gold, white and blue armor.

G explained, "We have come to you this day to see if this gentleman, named X, can help join your ranks to defeat the demon army."

Michael looked over X from head to toe. "He does not look like much. What can you do kid?"

G looked at X. "X, show him."

X took a deep breath and closed his eyes. When he opened them, he wore armor that was gold, red and black.

Michael laughed. "Seriously, we can all do that. Show me something I can use or stop wasting my time."

X closed his eyes once more then when he opened them, he had an all-black rapier in his hand.

Michael was no longer laughing. "That's a pretty fancy blade. How 'bout a friendly spar? Let's see what you really got. Follow me."

MICHEAL spread his wings and launched upwards. G and X followed. MICHAEL landed in a vacant field near by the base he felt as if they might need some space. X and G landed not too far away.

MICHAEL drew his sword from his sheath engraved with gold lettering and Roman numerals then took his stance. "Ok kid, charge at me."

X ran at Michael with all the speed he could muster slashing the sword at Michael with a direct hit, but Michael did not move. X felt a tap on his shoulder and turning around was punched in the face. As falling back, he felt a hand grabbing the collar of his armor then flinging him into the sky, where he was met again by Michael's speed. Michael executed a perfect flip kick, sending X back into the dirt. X was in pain and could not track his speed at all. Had this been a real fight, he would be dead by now for sure, he thought. Still, X was not ready to give up just yet. He closed his eyes to listen so he could track the speed. At the slightest sound from his right he guarded, he swung, and his sword luckily meeting Michael's blade.

"A response!" Michael said. "I was waiting to see when you would react."

"I'm not done yet, even though you're clearly kicking my ass."

"Ass whoopin' ain't over yet."

Michael smacked X's sword away from his hands then threw a heavy right punch. X dodged it. Michael then swung his sword but missed. X was getting faster, and Michael was in disbelief. He then began to swing repeatedly but missed each time. Michael threw down his sword. "Don't get cocky."

X did not reply but rather stopped in his tracks. Michael ran at X and threw a power-charged punch, striking X right in his chest, but X did not move. Michael felt a tap on his shoulder and turning about was met by a punch. While falling back, he felt the hand of X on the collar of his armor then was pulled into a rolling toss falling straight on his back. When he came to, X was standing over him with his blade to his neck. "This match is over."

Laughing, Michael rose, with the sword piercing through his neck and ghosting through the rest of the sword and X's body. "This is far from over." Standing behind X and charging up his fist with power, X moved dodging a powerful punch that upon hitting the ground caused a tremor. X rolled off to the side in awe at Michael's power.

Michael disappeared with great speed then reappeared in front of X, who then threw another punch of his own, only for his fist to be caught by Michaels left hand and then being punched with his right with another fist full of power right to the gut of X. Still holding on to X's fist, Michael began to spin his his own body around then released, flinging X's body into a tree snapping it in half. X felt a sharp amount of pain and thought, "Man this guy is getting serious."

X tried to rise but began to cough up some blood. His pride would not let him stay down, though. Looking up at Michael, he thought, "Damn, this guy is pretty powerful, but I think I can do better than that." Bringing himself to one knee, his body began to glow. He reached his hand out for his weapon, and it flew to his hand. Rising to both feet, his eyes also began to glow, and he said, "Let's finish this."

Michael was astonished. No one had ever survived this long against him. X disappeared then reappeared in front of Michael with his rapier slicing at Michael so fast then sheathing the sword at the same time Michael's armor shattered into pieces. X grabbed Michael by the throat and charged his fist with power. He lightly shoved it into Michael's face. Michael's body flew across the field until finally smashing into a giant boulder, his body indented. X appeared in front of him, charging his blade for a final attack then suddenly G stepped in between the two.

"Ok, we get it, yours is larger," G said. "This was only supposed to be a spar, cool it."

X powered down, Michael fainted, and the field was quiet. X also blacked out.

❧ᎦᏋᎦᎦ Chapter 8 ❧ᎦᏋᎦᎦ

Awakened by the sound of a strange humming in his ear, Y was startled to find himself bound from limb to limb by chains and set ablaze with fire. He thought to himself, "I have not been chained up like this since that one hooker in Texas." Then the humming became louder, he began to look around. He was surely in another section of hell but where? He could see furniture that looked like a bed and many vanity mirrors all over the walls of the cavern but none were actual pictures of anyone. Candles were lit everywhere, so whoever it was, they did not mind being seen.

As the humming ended, he heard a voice from behind. "It's a damn shame you have such a bounty on your head. You're kinda cute."

Y could not recognize the voice only that it was female. "I wish I could say the same for you, but I can't see who's talking."

Quickly changing her form into something Y was familiar with, she stepped before him as a dark-haired, gorgeous caramel-skinned woman with the figure of that of a Coke bottle wearing a red dress that wrapped tight around every curve, and matching red heels to complement.

Y dropped his head and laughed. "Jackpot! Are you sure this is hell?"

She pulled a large spiked paddle out from behind her back

"Fuck," he said.

"You want to tell me why such a large bounty is out for you?"

"Nope. Even if I told you, it would not matter."

She cocked back the paddle for a mighty swing

"Don't do that. It's just going to piss me off. I never was a fan of the paddles or this whole tie-me-up shit." Rolling one eye to the back of his head, he summoned Squylir.

Squylir appeared. "Yes, what's going on out there?"

18

"Squylir, who is this crazy, kinky bitch?"

"She appears to be a succubus. Did you two—"

"Does it look like my pants are down?"

"Who are you talking to?" she said with a mighty swing of the paddle to the backside of Y.

Cringing in pain, Y dropped his head once more with his eye rolling back forward. "I told you, I'm not a fan of the paddles."

The chains that bound Y began to turn into ice, and when he lifted his head they shattered, sending Y falling to the floor.

The succubus looked confused and amazed at the same time. "I think I see why that bounty is so high for your head."

Y rose to his feet. "Look lady, I got some shit to do. Now if you're going to try to kill me or whatever, hurry up."

"My name is not 'lady,' it's Vimarra, and I was not going to kill you, just turn you in for the reward."

"And what is this reward?"

"Better living. It's hell – you still have to pay rent down here, ya know, so a huge amount of money plus more frequent trips to the world of the living. I'm a succubus, we kinda need that... Do you have a name?"

"It's Y, you freak, and if you're not going to try to kill me, I guess I'll be leaving. Oh yeah, you're not getting away with that paddle shit." Y snapped his fingers.

Vimarra suddenly was suspended in midair in chains. She instantly was mad but also turned on by his power. "What are you going to do to me?"

"I'm leaving. Like I said, I have shit to do."

Watching Y walk away into the darkness, she yelled, "Take me with you! I'll guide you to where you need to go." Waiting for a response, she thought she was left for dead, then she heard a snap and the chains falling off.

Y yelled from the darkness, "Catch up, ya freak!"

❧❦◡❧❦ Chapter 9 ❧❦◡❧❦

Waking up in a daze and in a confusion, Michael stood over X. "Time to wake up."

X yawned. "Have I earned the right to train with you, so you can show me how to do all that cool stuff?"

Michael was confused. "How can I show you something you already know how to do. You are an angel, right?"

X balled up his fist and imagined energy coming from it as looking up at Michael. "It's like if I imagine it, it will happen – is that how it works for you guys?"

Michael was stunned. "If you're not creating this power with angelic energy then how is this possible?"

Gabriel stepped in. "He's not like us. Grab his hand, and you will see that it is warm."

Michael grabbed X's wrist and dropped it in disbelief. "What are you?"

Gabriel began to explain to Michael about the entity that dwells inside of X's body is allowing his spirit to stay fused with the body therefore he was able still walk among the world of the living as well.

Michael was astonished and turned to X. "How did you die?"

X, hesitating to answer the question, was interrupted by the footsteps of another walking into the room. "Are we ready to begin daily training, sir?"

Michael replied, "Private, gather the rest of the squad. We have got a new recruit."

Looking at Michael, X nodded. Gabriel, looking at Michael, nodding as well.

Michael only shook his head. "I don't know what you're nodding, for messenger boy." Then looking back at X, he said, "Let's go. We have some work to do. There are some folks I want you to meet."

Michael began to walk out, and X and Gabriel followed, walking around the base seeing more and more angel soldiers flying in for daily drills. The base was huge. Although it did not have any tanks or choppers, it did have a firing range, hospital and lots of different areas for different drills and situations. Michael led them past a large group of soldiers.

X started pointing at the mass of soldiers. "Aren't we supposed to meet with them?"

Michael kept walking and did not reply until arriving at the door of a giant hangar. "Welcome to the angel elite," he said and opened the massive hangar door.

X saw a group of five angels all wearing armor that was black and gold.

"You will be training with the best of the best, kid," Michael said. "This unit was designed as a tactical squad of the most talented angels whose power is above average. None of them match mine, of course, but these gifted five will teach and help get you where you need to be."

Michael introduced "Bird," who stood at 6'2" 210 pounds, "Black Jack" standing at 6'4" 200 pounds, "Waters" at 5'11 200 pounds, and "Ref" standing at 5"11 150 pounds.

One was missing, though.

⧼⧽ Chapter 10 ⧼⧽

Traveling alongside Y, Vimarra was eager to know why he could not see in the dark in hell "You are a demon aren't you?"

Y did not answer.

Vimarra went on. "Demons use a special—"

Y interrupted. "I don't care." Snapping his fingers, he illuminated the path with more torches through another cold cavern of hell.

At last, they came upon a landmark that was familiar to Vimarra. "This is Blood Lake. If I'm not mistaken a spawning circle is nearby?"

"What is a spawning circle?"

Vimarra glanced around. "Look there. It's basically a summoning circle the demon army uses as a portal down here for instant transportation to a certain area or areas."

Y's face turned pale as he dropped his jaw. "So you mean to tell me that we are walking basically into a trap. Do you know how to use one of the circles? Can you get us out of here?"

Vimarra shook her head. "I've never had to use one before."

While they tried to come up with a plan, several of the circles around Blood Lake began to glow causing the blood in the lake to boil and bubble. Four demon guards materialized from the portals. These demons were different from the first one Y fought – they are a lot smaller and had the bodies of a man with wings and other features of animals such as a lion's mane, the scales of a crocodile, or the beak of an eagle. Y readied himself, for battle clapping his hands together creating a katana for himself then snapping once more to gain a pair of wings of his own. He took flight.

Vimarra was excited to see Y geared up and ready, and she too readied herself for battle in her natural demon form. She ripped off the dress, revealing a black bra and matching bikini bottoms. A tail fell from her lower back and horns began growing out of her skull. Her delicate hands turned into razor sharp claws, and her demons wings spread, as she too took flight to meet the guards over Blood Lake.

One of the guards spoke. "We're here to collect the body of the one who chooses to overthrow the Dark King."

Y replied, "You're here to take my body, huh? Well, come take it."

The guard spoke again. "Kill the succubus as well."

Vimarra snarled. "Bring it on."

Two of the guards rushed for Y and two at Vimarra. Vimarra charged at one of the guards with great speed, ramming one of them directly in the chest, sending him splashing into Blood Lake. The other guard pulled out a chain, and throwing it wrapped it tight around her. She glared at the beast guard, putting him under hypnosis, which caused him to release chains, Vimarra calmly glided over and punched a hole through his chest. "Piece of cake," she said.

Meanwhile, Y charged at one of the beast guards at full speed but was interrupted by the sight of more guards coming through the portals. Snapping his fingers, a suitcase appeared by each portal. One of the beast guards in front of Y took in a deep breath to breathe fire at him.

Vimarra swooped in to tackle Y and rolled out of the fireball's way.

"I don't need your help – get out of my way!" Y shouted.

"Fine be crispy," Vimarra said.

The beast guard took in another deep breath. Vimarra aimed her index finger shooting her claw right into the guard's throat. The last guard did not move. Y approached with caution.

The guard seemed to be in a possessed state then spoke. "You think you have won? The best is yet to come for you, spy of heaven."

Y replied, "'Spy of heaven,' what does that mean?"

"So heaven has made its move. They will regret trying to take my kingdom." The portals began to expel more guards.

Y laughed. "You think I didn't see that coming?" Clapping his hands, the suitcase opened to reveal mini-machine guns locking onto and firing at each guard as they shot out of the portal.

Vimarra watched in awe as each guard was turned to ash. "It's almost like like a fireworks show."

Y looked. "Ok, that's just creepy."

The possessed guard laughed while its body made a slow descent into the boiling blood lake.

Y scratched his head. "Let's get out of here."

The blood lake began to overflow, as Vimarra and Y ran into more of the unknown. Blood Lake, also used as sacrificial pool of summoning, suddenly began to glow, shooting a beam of light into the air creating a portal to the world of the living. A building-sized evil clown climbed out of the portal and began to terrorize New York City, spitting acid killing hundreds instantly.

❧❧ Chapter 11 ❧❧

With the introduction of the angel elite, X was excited to meet his new teachers.

Ref raised his fist. "X, you will be training with me first. The faster you apply my skill, the better."

X was intrigued. "What is your skill?"

"Elements."

X was excited. "I'm ready."

Michael nodded to Ref then was interrupted by another angel elite member walking in by the name of Grid.

"Michael, we have a problem."

Michael looked at Grid, already pissed off that he was late. "What is it now?"

Grid looked at X then whispered to Michael, who pointed to Black Jack and told him to go with Grid and "Handle that." Grid and Black Jack left the warehouse, and Michael told Ref to continue.

Ref looked at X. "If our Intel is correct, you can create anything you need or mimic power if you want, so you want to try or mimic this."

Ref clenched his fist then calmed his mind. Taking a deep breath, a force began to stir up around his body, and the element of lightning was surged throughout his body. His eyes glowed blue then began to shift into red as his body was engulfed in flames. As his body began to cool, his eyes turned blue, and he washed away the flames with water then brown to control the earth beneath him, lifting himself onto a platform made of rock.

X was amazed. "Whoa, that's insane." He closed his eyes to replicate Ref's power. His body was on fire but not what he expected.

As X felt the burn, Ref put out the flames. "Remember that being an angel our faith drives our power," Ref said. "Try again. This time, put your real passion into it."

X closed his eyes not only to concentrate but to find his drive and his motivation.

Ref could see his hands start to change, as if they were heating up. "That's it, keep it up."

X began to have have a flashback of the whole reason he was on that rooftop, remembering the pressures of being alive and what it is find self-value.

Ref could see that this time X's body was on fire, but it was not burning him. "Open your eyes, X." He grabbed X by the shoulder. "That's good, not bad. You're a fast learner. Now let me see some lightning."

X calmly clenched his fist he put out the flame and let his motivation take charge, sending a shock of electricity through his body and illuminating the hangar.

Bird stepped forward. "Cool light show, Ref, but now it's my turn. X, what good is all that elemental shit without applying it to a weapon?" Bird pulled out two pistols tossing one to X. "See those targets over there? I want all head shots with pinpoint accuracy."

X had never held a gun before Bird looked at Ref. "Do me a favor –"

Ref already knew charging both pistols with lighting Bird looked back at X. "I like to stir shit up a bit. Now let's see it."

X fired a shot, hitting one of the targets taking its whole leg off.

Bird's face was in tears with laughter. "Ok, try it again. I'm not giving you a speech like Ref. Just point and shoot 'til you eventually get a head shot."

It took 35 shots until X was finally able to land a headshot.

Ref nudged Bird who was half-asleep. "What do you want him to do now? He got one."

Bird took out a switch out of his pocket dropping more targets down. "Ref, you know what to do."

Ref charged the targets with lightning, and they became animate.

Bird laughed. "See these new targets? All I have to say is destroy them, and Waters can take the next form of training from here." Bird failed to mention that the targets were going to try to hurt him.

X nodded. "I'll do my best."

Ref and Bird walked back to where Waters and Michael stood. X was surrounded by the four targets one of the targets shot electricity at him X was caught off guard by the hit and was blasted back into the arms of another target, which had him locked in tight with a bear hug. X began to panic as the other three targets began to shoot lightning at him sending multiple shocks through his system. As X felt the pain of his shocks, his eyes glowed yellow then he began to absorb the lightning with his own while absorbing the shocks X closed his eyes, creating a wall between the three targets and himself and the one that had him locked in, quickly heated up his body melting the target that had him locked in its arms, then without hesitation snapping his fingers creating a shotgun infusing the shells with fire. The next three targets came bursting through the wall. Pumping the shotgun and taking aim, he blasted the target to his left in the face, shattering its head into pieces. The rest of the target disappeared. X was excited, but with his excitement, his eyes and body began to glow whitish blue.

Bird looked at Ref. "What element is that?"

Ref shrugged. "I don't know."

Michael said, "That's not an element. He's going into a rage-like mode. Looks like depending upon his attitude it's triggered."

X's body began to form an aura as he stopped in his tracks almost daring the targets to come for him. The two targets ran up to X punching him in the face and in the gut but with no effect. X caught one of the punches, grabbing the target's arm and swinging its body into the other target then pulling the targets arm in close to himself X punched into the targets head turning it into powder then aiming the shotgun once more, he fired a single shot at the remaining target, flawlessly landing the shot in its head.

Bird's, Ref's and Waters' jaws were dropped.

Michael smiled at Bird and Ref. "Don't move. He has to calm himself."

X's body stood motionless then fell inanimate.

❧❦❧ Chapter 12 ❧❦❧

Coming out of the portal from heaven, Grid and Black Jack immediately charged for the giant evil clown. Grid flew with great speed like a meteor smashed into the head of the clown, the head bursting like a balloon, and sent smaller clowns flying everywhere. Grid shook his head. "I fucking hate clowns."

"Don't trip," Black Jack said then waved his staff opening up a portal back into hell. The portal began to suck the clowns back into the depths of hell.

While the portal was open, Grid noticed Vimarra and Y fleeing for safety. "Black Jack, did you see that dude? Weird style of wings for a demon. It's almost like they were made of energy."

Black Jack nodded. "Yeah, let's get back to Michael and report it."

Opening another portal back to heaven, Black Jack and Grid flew in to return to the training of X.

With the demon army hot on their tail, Y and Vimarra were looking to put some ground between themselves and the demon army. Vimarra looking back at the climbing numbers behind them. "What are we going to do?" she said. "If we take on that many, we will surely be killed."

Y snapped his fingers and laughed as layers of walls of different types came crashing down behind them. Rolling one eye to the back of his skull, he looked for Squylir. "I know you're in there," Y said.

Squylir appeared. "The only way to escape is to get out of hell, but you don't possess the know how to get out."

Y laughed. "I could easily create a way to earth."

Squylir laughed, too. "Then they will pull your ass right back down 'til your dead." Squylir was silent for a moment. "If you let me out, I will take you to a dimension where they can't find you your and your sex toy."

Y thought about Squylir trying to kill him. "I don't know, asshole; if let you out, I'm not turning my back to your sneaky ass."

"Fine, but your barriers are running out."

Like a contact lens, Y began to fish Squylir out of his eye.

Vimarra was disgusted. "What the hell are you doing?" Squylir was extracted from Y's eye, and Vimarra looked down at him. "Who the hell are you?"

Squylir ignored her and pulled a key from inside of his robe. "Follow me; stay close."

Y and Vimarra nodded. Squylir pulled back reality and space, opening up a portal of rare proportions into a dimension unknown to many angel or demon.

Vimarra was amazed. "Where is this place?"

"This is obviously not heaven or hell, so stop the questions already," Squylir said. "You are in the domain of the reaper."

Y could not help but notice that millions of floating pains were all around the domain. "Looks like your boss keeps an eye out for those souls."

Squylir then became nervous not knowing the consequence of bringing the two to the domain even though it meant his freedom

Y suddenly noticed his own pain, as it stood out more than the others. "Hey, check out that asshole." Then Y noticed the pain of another guy. "Squylir who's this dude?"

Squylir shuddered to answer, again thinking about the consequences, then suddenly the portal to the domain opened once again and the Reaper appeared.

𝒶𝒸𝒸𝒹𝒶 Chapter 13 𝒶𝒸𝒸𝒹𝒶

Two hours passed as X's body depleted all of its energy. Coming to X asked, "What happened?"

Waters was beside him with his hands in a prayer-like state. "I replenished your energy. Now get up so I can teach you how to heal yourself and others if need be."

Just as Waters began showing X his techniques Grid, Black Jack stormed in loudly with Grid yelling, "We handled that shit."

The rest of the elite looking over at all the commotion. Michael quickly scolded them. "Will you shut the hell up? X is trying to concentrate."

Grid looking at Ref, shrugged "what," and walked over to Ref. "You'll never guess what we saw."

Michael interrupted. "Well hurry up and spill the beans."

Grid began to explain about how the fight went and what was witnessed after.

Michael wasn't shocked at all. "So there are two of them?"

Black Jack raised his staff to show Michael a look into hell, but when he opened the portal, nothing was there. "I know what we saw, Michael."

Waters was finished teaching his techniques. "Ok I'm done, who's up next?"

Grid stepped forward, but at that very moment a portal opened, pulling him into it.

Black Jack laughed. "So you thought."

Michael shook his head. "Whatever. Get to it."

Black Jack began to explain to X that the opening of portals can help him get out of some sticky situations and that he needs to be able to manipulate them to be able to pull forces in and to expel forces out, raising his staff once more. Grid fell out of the portal he opened, got up, and yelled, "You dick, I was next!"

Black Jack laughed. "Ok fine, we will work more with portals In a second."

Grid stepped up again. "Tell me how fast are you." X began to answer the question but was interrupted by Grid. "How strong are you?"

X began once more. "Well, I once lifted a—"

Grid interrupted again. "Does not matter. None of that does not matter without stamina. With angelic stamina, which is part of what I will teach you, it will be tough for you to become tired for me. It's all about shifting your energy to where it is needed most at the time. Let's all race; yo, Ref, make a track."

Ref began but X stopped him. "Allow me, Ref." X clapped turning the whole hangar into track with clay and even the lines chalked and ready with numbers and starting points. Ref was cool with that. Stepping back, X walked over to to a starting position. "Ok, let's do this."

Grid looked at Michael smirking while walking to his starting position.

Bird took out a pistol. "First one around the track wins."

The pistol fired, and X and Grid took off like lightning bolts.

Grid was impressed by the speed of X. "You really did fight, Michael, because that's exactly how fast he is," he said to X. Then Grid's legs began to move a lot more rapidly, and he vanished.

X stopped in his tracks. "What the fuck?" X looked around and saw Grid at the starting line. In disbelief, X said, "Tell me how."

Grid flashed back before him. 'Revert and direct your energy to where you need it most. Think of it this way – the blood cells in your body rush to where you need them most; same concept, except with angelic kinetic energy, the same way we all control the power we command our faith, and our drive commands that power to where you need it most."

X began to focus his angelic energy. He could feel the energy circulating around his body, realized the same rules applied to strength and stamina. X felt as if he was ready for whatever came his way.

Black Jack stepped forward. "I'll take over. The opening and closing of these portals is very important. NOT many angels or demons can use this ability, but the ones that can are very important. Being able to travel anywhere instantly has its advantages. Also, one more thing about me – I can control the physics of the situation. Gravity plays a huge role in any battle. If your enemies are off balance, they can be taken out easily." Black Jack opening a portal released a hell spawn from another dimension.

X was amazed. "What is that?"

Black Jack replied, "This is a creature of hell. I'm using him as a test subject. I've been in trial with a new ability of mine, which is opening portals to the unknown or rather dimensions no one or rare have been to."

X was astonished. "Wow, teach me that."

"I wish I could, but it's still in development."

❧☙❧ Chapter 14 ❧☙❧

Floating out of the portal, the Reaper glided over to the group of three, his nightshade of a body easily standing more than seven feet tall. With a robe made of dark energy draping his body in a dark shroud, he had more human-like features with a sash of silver skulls across his chest. His scythe, with a large black curved blade, glowed with the same dark energy and shroud. "Squylir, why have you returned to my domain without completing your task?"

Squylir remains silent.

"Upon that, you bring others here as if you rule this domain explain your actions."

Y spoke up. "Squylir got us out of a jam."

The Reaper turned to Y. As the mist of his shroud touched Y's face, it instantly became cold. "Who told you to speak? I have not addressed you yet. I know, I know – you feel important." Scanning Y's body with the scythe to see who he was, in shock he almost lost grip of the scythe. "Squylir, why have you bought him here? You have put us all in danger."

Y laughed. "Suddenly I'm a threat to you, huh?"

The Reaper remained quiet.

"I have some questions for you, asshole, starting with why I'm being monitored so closely –

me and that other guy."

"You and that guy are to remain apart. We do not know the consequence of the reaction between you two."

Y scratched his head. "Who is he, and who is we?"

The Reaper pointed to X's screen. "He is the alpha to your omega, the ultimate good to your evil."

"You mean to tell me that we are some kind of weapons?"

33

"Not weapons but with God-like power the ultimate power of creation. Anything seems virtually possible, starting with the cause of the Big Bang."

Y scratched his head again. "So I made all this?"

The Reaper laughed. "The entities that dwells inside of you both are responsible but still through the power of God."

Y began to laugh uncontrollably. "So you mean to tell me I'm I'm a fucking bomb with unlimited power?"

The Reaper floating quietly. "If you plan on destroying this universe, I am not going to let you leave this domain."

❧❦❧ Chapter 15 ❧❦❧

The Dark King was not satisfied as news spread of the escape of who he thought to be the spy of heaven, angry at the fact of failure he was not going to be made a mockery of ordering the killing of many demons in order to make a summoning of a creatures called the demon-skin masked horsemen. The demon bodies fell into the lake one by one until the Blood Lake began to boil, shooting a beam of light connecting from hell this time into heaven interrupting the training of X.

The sky of heaven turned red from the light of the summoning. Two men rode out of the beam of light wearing dark silver metal armor sitting upon two skeleton steeds wearing masks made of demon skin to hide their identity. One carried a massive battle-axe; the other carried a dark silver metal bow and arrows. Upon riding out of the light, they began to immediately terrorize the citizens of heaven.

The Dark King laughed, as spreading his wings. "Toss me out of heaven will ya; guess they forgot I still had a key to the door."

Hearing the screams and destruction, the angel military sprang into action, but the horsemen were not intimidated, as they tore the military apart, hacking and slashing the angel army down. One of the horsemen rode down to the ground and planted his axe firmly into the soil creating a massive summoning circle, which immediately spawned hundreds of demons of different types pouring into heaven.

The battle had begun between angels and demons.

The training of X was over as he and the angel elite, including Michael, were just arriving to the battle.

❧❧❧ Chapter 16 ❧❧❧

Y laughed as the Reaper warned him of his threat to leave his realm and wreak havoc on earth, heaven and hell. The Reaper's scythe began to glow with purple and black flames. The fire from the scythe spread throughout the Reaper's body. Raising the scythe, the Reaper flung a huge amount of energy toward Y. Y yawned, and snapping his fingers a fire hose appeared in his arms blasting water at the flames coming his way. It did not extinguish the flames engulfing Y's body, though.

The Reaper laughed. "What's the matter, can't take the heat?" He charged at Y and pulled back his scythe to finish him.

As the Reaper swung, Vimarra tackled Y out of the way. "What are you doing, Y, snap out of it, it's an illusion!" she shouted.

Y realized why he could not extinguish the flames. "But it felt so real." He was a bit shook up.

Countering with great speed, the Reaper was able to appear in back of the two. He struck Vimarra unconscious with the butt of the scythe, and said to her fallen body, "Do not interfere." He pulled back the scythe for another swing.

Snapping his fingers, Y met the scythe with the edge of a heavy sword. The Reaper reached beyond the scythe and the great sword to touch Y, who knew with one touch to his skin the fight would be over. "Oh no you don't," Y said as winking one eye.

His body suddenly was wrapped in latex.

"Doesn't just protect against STD's, I hope," Y said.

As the hand of the Reaper grazed Y's face, the latex dissolved. Y pushed the Reaper back with the great sword, which also began to develop a patina. Y realized it was going to take a lot more than just his creation powers to beat the Reaper. Snapping his fingers to give him time, he thought he would be able to slow the Reaper down, but the Reaper still was able to move.

The Reaper floated to him. "You have no chance of beating me. I was wrong to put you high upon the top tier."

Y felt insulted. "I'll beat you, you think with that stupid scythe that's all it takes to beat me." The great sword began to glow as Y's hate began to be fueled. Y' eyes began to glow a bright red. As a bloody tear rolled down out of his eye socket and down his cheek, his body began to transform, as the horns a ram spiraled out of his skull.

The Reaper realized Y had tapped into a form of his own demon-like powers. Y's hands turned into claws and a tail pierced through the back of his pants, slamming the great sword into the ground causing fire to erupt from the cracks of the floor. Flames began surrounding the Reaper, who tapped the butt of the scythe into the ground. It instantly put out the flames, but Y wasted no time leaping into the air, and with the massive sword came down above the Reaper to slice him. The Reaper ghost through the blade, though, and grabbing Y by the collar of his shirt threw him into the wall. Charging up the scythe, he launched a huge amount of energy in the form of a skull at Y. Y managed to block it, but the explosion that came after was not pleasant. Y's body fell to the floor. The Reaper thought he would seize the opportunity to finish him off glided over to collect the soul. As reaching his hand toward the back of Y's head, though, Y lifted his head and shot a concentrated energy blast out of his eyes directly at the hand, obliterating it and the forearm.

The Reaper shrieked back in pain. "You bastard!"

Y kept shooting more beams. The one-armed Reaper showed his skill deflecting every beam with the scythe then opened a gate to an unknown dimension and released an alien-like creature into the domain.

"Buy me some time," the Reaper said to the creature, but to his surprise, Y had stored an enormous amount of dark energy in his sword, an amount that began to overflow killing the alien instantly as it tried to attack.

Holding the sword firmly, Y ran at the Reaper fully charged. The Reaper tried to muster enough energy to match Y's amount, and one amount of energy began to overwhelm the other, causing a huge explosion. Y flew back into the wall, and the Reaper turned into ash, the scythe stuck into ground from the impact.

Hurt and exhausted, Y turned back into his human form. Grabbing the scythe, he pulled it out of the hole.

Vimarra awakened. "What happened – why are you holding the Reaper's scythe and where is he?"

Y was silent at first. "Isn't it obvious? He's dead."

Squylir appeared. "You have killed my master. Does this mean I am free to do as I please?"

"Hell no," Y said. "You will be my scout along with the other guy."

Vimarra was amazed by the power of the scythe. "Do you know what that thing is capable of? It has the power to travel through different dimensions and through different realms with ease."

"Other realms and dimensions?" Y said. "Looks like we're going back to hell."

❧❦☙❧ Chapter 17 ❧❦☙❧

As the battle for heaven raged, the demon-skin masked horsemen were met by the angel elite. X was eager to try out his new powers, but there was a standstill at their arrival.

Michael landed first. "I don't know or care what this shit is about, but you two aren't leaving here alive."

The larger horseman laughed. "It is you who is going to die in your own house. We're just here to see to it that the job is done. We will kill the spy of heaven along with all the angels for the Dark Kingdom. What do you think of this, brother?"

The other horseman nodded. "We will rule this sector."

Michael laughed. "X and Ref, take care of these clowns. We'll take out the other demons."

X and Ref nodded. "We got this."

Michael and the others began to attack the other demons in waves. X, Ref and the horsemen stood still. A calm wind blew by, and a leaf floated to the ground calmly in the middle of the four. The larger of the horsemen let out a war cry and charged his bone steed straight for Ref. Ref charged his fist with lightning, beginning to throw bolts at the horseman but missed for the steed's speed was great. The other horseman began to shoot dark energy-filled arrows from his bow. X smiled as he began to walk toward the horseman, creating dual desert eagles and and charging the bullets with different elements while shooting the arrows out of the sky.

Ref was amazed but kept his focus on the larger horseman before him. As the horseman came extremely close to swinging at him with the giant battle axe, Ref dodged the attack, turning one fist to water and the other to dirt, and slapping them together splashing mud into the horseman's eye. It had no effect. The horseman grabbing Ref by the neck and dragging through the soil like a plow through dirt. The speed of his horse was too fast to react.

X could see that Ref was in trouble. Shooting down the last arrow with great speed, he swung to back of his opponent, snatched the bow out of his hands, and created a metal bat. Cracking the horseman in the face, he shot the other one in the shoulder. The Desert Eagle caused the horseman to lose his grip on Ref's neck. Ref charged his whole body with lightning, shocking the horseman, forcing him to release Ref, who tucked and rolled. Giving a thumbs up, X nodded and threw the bat his way. In midair, the bat turned into a shield. Ref caught it then turned back to the horseman whose axe was in mid-swing. The shield blocked the force of the axe, sent Ref flying back into X.

"Dude, seriously," X said.

Ref laughed. "My bad. Grab my arms; I have an idea." X did. "Now spin and generate electricity."

X began to spin fast in midair. Ref's eyes began to turn grey, as the spin turned into a tornado charged with electricity moving toward the horsemen. The first horseman tried to escape, but the force pulled him in and trapping him. The other horseman threw his axe into the tornado thinking that it would stop the force; the axe cut right through the force ripping right through the other horsemen and out the other side.

X in surprise said, "Did not see that coming."

Ref smiled. "Let's finish this."

X could feel Ref hands heating up; they were so hot they burned, so he let go, shooting Ref as a fireball into the last horseman, causing a massive explosion upon impact. When the smoke cleared, X could see Ref posing.

"What are you doing?" X said.

"What? This is my finished stance." Ref's body cooled off.

"Let's go help the others."

As they were about to take off, X looked off to his right and saw Michael and the other elite.

Michael asked, "Help us with what?" Grid, Black Jack and Waters smirked behind him.

Suddenly a portal opened above the elite. Michael looked at Black Jack.

Black Jack was puzzled. "Sir, I don't know."

Long arms began to reach out of the portal, pulling in Black Jack. "What is going on?" he shouted.

They tried to fight off the arms, but it was no use. Black Jack had been taken.

⟨⟨⟨ Chapter 18 ⟩⟩⟩

Holding the scythe tightly in both hands, Y raised it over his head. "Take us to hell."

Vimarra and Squylir looked at each other and began to laugh.

"You really think that's going to work with a powerful weapon like that?" Vimarra said.

A portal begins to open into hell, and Y smirked. "See? Shut up. As a matter fact, shut the hell up. Let's go."

As the three walked into the portal, each of their faces were surprised yet stunned. The domain of the Reaper was quiet; all that remained was a pile of ash that was the former Reaper.

As the portal to hell closed, another portal opened, throwing Black Jack onto the floor of the Reaper's domain. Black Jack fell right into the ashes with a confused look upon his face. "Where am I?"

Arriving back into the depths of hell, Y looked to Vimarra. "Ok succubus, where are we going?"

"Finally letting me take control, daddy?" She walked ahead. "Y, can you see down here yet?"

Y for some reason could see. "Yeah, actually." Not fully back in his human form, Y sensed the demon powers he activated were the reason he could see. "So where are we?"

Vimarra looked around at the landmarks. "We're pretty close to the basement."

"What is the basement?"

Squylir chimed in. "It's the nickname for the Dark Kingdom because it's so far deep in the underground of hell."

Y's jaw dropped. "So you're telling me that hell, which seems to be nothing more but a maze of caverns and darkness, is ruled by some guy living comfortably In a basement? This is just not how I pictured hell."

Vimarra and Squylir laughed again. "You're funny Y."

Getting more upset, Y began to walk toward the entrance of the basement. "Something about this seems too easy."

"Don't say things like that," Vimarra said. "Last time we got chased by that demon hoard."

Squylir butted in. "I don't think that he will need an army for the basement. There are far nastier things in the basement to deal with I'm sure."

"Now I'm anxious to know what's down there," Y said, "because you assholes keep talking and aren't walking."

Walking a half mile to the entrance, the gate was literally a giant hole with stairs. Once they got closer to the bottom, they could see light, which was strange because everything outside the entrance was pitch black. Stepping into the light, Vimarra hissed.

Y looked at her. "Do you sense something?"

Vimarra looked around as they walked into what looked like to be the walls of a castle, well lit with torches on the walls with paintings and things made of gold and silver everywhere. While walking upon a corridor, they noticed a dining hall scattered across the table is a vast array of different foods. Everything looked delicious.

Y looked at all the food. "Damn, hell has a hell of a cook."

Vimarra licked her lips. "That cheesecake looks so delightful, it would be a sin not to eat it." Noticing Squylir about to take a big bite from a ham, she slapped it from his mouth. "What the fuck do you think you are doing? Do you realize this could be a trap?"

As they both turned around to see Y stuffing his face, the room began to shake, and the floor began to open. As the only walkable path was the dinner table, Y yelled, "Everyone on the fucking table!"

They did as he said. Everything below the table was boiling hot acid.

Vimarra began to notice the ceiling opening as well. "Now what?"

Looking above, they began to notice giant faces and eyes in the darkness suddenly a massive hand holding a fork hovered above them.

"Fucking run, scatter!" Y yelled.

Giant forks and knives began to slam into the table all around them. Y was dodging the forks with ease, and Vimarra was just showing off until one of the forks caught a piece of her wing pulling her down to the table. Y clapped his hands, creating a cork-like barrier above them so it would take the other forks and knives a bit of time to pierce through. Vimarra was pinned down, and Y was trying to think quickly. He took a deep breath and began to shoot flames from his mouth heating up the fork as he expected it to melt; the forks and knives began to almost tear through the cork. When the fork was fully melted, Y and Squylir pulled Vimarra free. Wiping the liquid away from her wing, Y felt that it was plastic.

"What the fuck, plastic?" he said. "Those cheap bastards! This must be hell."

Y raised his hand, as if he was going to strike Vimarra. Instead a bandage appeared on the wing.

"Ok, let's move," he said. "No more fancy shit, just move; we're almost to the exit." Snapping his fingers, the cork disappeared everyone scattered once more with the forks and knives raining down.

Knowing they were made of plastic, Y and Vimarra began to shoot fire as they ran at the forks and knives. Squylir just stayed in Y's shadow.

Reaching the end of table and stumbling into the next room, they noticed everything was made of precious gems stones, gold, silver and the rarest metals known to man. This time, no one touched anything but upon being there the jewels began to fuse together in the form of jewel knights. Y blew fire once more, which was deflected by their shields which were made of diamonds and so we're there swords. Y readied the scythe and charged into battle. Vimarra followed, but Squylir turned into his shadow form and entered one of the jewel knights suits for his own possession. "This is nice," he said then also charged into battle.

Y began to swing the scythe at the jewel knights, not making a scratch with the blade. The jewel knights began to fight back, armed with swords made of the strongest steel known to man. Y was able to dodge their attacks easily with his speed; so was Vimarra. They did not even realize that Squylir was there he had not attempted to attack just yet.

Without landing a hit on both sides, the jewel knights became furious. They reverted into a jewel mush then molding and fusing created a jewel centipede, of which the legs were made of the same sharp steel as the swords. It had those same blades for the pinchers. Once done with its transformation. It burrowed underground.

No one gave chase. They stood still to see where is would strike. Then the ground underneath them shook violently, knocking Squylir in his armor off balance. Once the armor hit the floor, the centipede came up with Squylir in its pinchers. As it snapped the armor in two, Squylir slithered out, just barely escaping.

Y noticed that many of the larger pieces of its armor was made of diamonds. "Vimarra, I have idea – I want you to attack those larger diamond plates."

She nodded, and using her speed got in close. Y closed his eyes, and when they opened Vimarra's claws and horns were made entirely of diamonds. She clawed at one of the plates on the chest of the centipede. Gold poured out in the form of liquid. Y's hunch was right. Sweeping his hand over the blade of the scythe, it turned to diamond, then he spread his wings taking flight at full speed to the centipede's head, he charged the scythe with his own energy. He struck the main plate. The centipede shattered instantly.

A door opened for the next chamber.

❧❦❧ Chapter 19 ❧❦❧

With the Black Jack's disappearance, the elite were left with questions but coming up with no answers.

Michael began to notice that some of the fallen angels and demons on the battlefield were still alive. "That's strange; I could have sworn I killed most of those bastards."

X was the only other angel that could open portals. "Maybe he was taken to hell, kidnapped."

"No, that's stupid. The devil would not want anything to do with him unless he's holding him for ransom, but we have not received any notice."

Gabriel walked up, suddenly acting unusually strange.

Michael looked at him. "What's wrong with you?"

"My master has fallen; the new master orders me to attack, but I will surely fail" Gabriel said.

Bird snapped his fingers in front of his face. "Who is your new master?"

"He who wields the scythe of the reaper." Gabriel took a small dagger out of his messenger bag. "Restrain me or I will attack!"

Michael laughed. "Messenger boy, stop playing around. We don't have time for –"

Gabriel leapt at Michael with the dagger. X quickly created a barrier between them then snapping his fingers encased Gabriel in a straitjacket. Gabriel dropped his head low as his eyes turned all black.

X turned to Michael. "Let's look on earth for Black Jack."

Opening a portal, they all leapt through. Upon arrival, the elite began their search, as X flew over his old house. He began to flashback to his old friends and family, remembering all of the good times he had when he was alive. He did not want to risk the chance of his family seeing him alive. It would probably freak them out, he thought as he flew off. He had another flashback to all the times he had hurt himself and things he had done in which he probably should have died. Maybe this entity has been protecting me longer than I thought, X wondered.

His thoughts were interrupted by a radio link message from Michael. "A portal has opened up near Roswell; get your ass here now."

X opening his own portal walked through into New Mexico. Seeing the other portal and the other elite, he asked, "What is it?"

Michael replied, "Don't know yet but the Dark King is pushing his luck."

Sitting upon his throne, the devil smirked.

X and the elite, in anticipation of seeing what would come from the portal, saw a swarm of bugs emerge. The bugs immediately attacked the elite with painful stings and bites, and they eliminated the bugs any way they could they free themselves.

Looking at the others, Michael said, "Everyone good? What the fuck was that about?"

Grid replied, "I don't know, but I'd fucking hate..." Grid began to dig in his ear as if something was in it.

Waters rushed over to Grid. "I don't see anything, but I'll..." Waters, too, began to dig in his ear, then Michael, and even Ref.

X was clueless. "What the hell is going on?" X wished he had X-ray specs. "Oh wait." Snapping his fingers, X could see that in each of their bodies hundreds of tiny bugs invaded their organs and were attaching themselves mainly to the nervous system and the spinal cord. "You guys, the bugs!"

Each one of the elite began to fall out of the sky then rolling on the ground in pain. Suddenly the pain and rolling stopped, and the bodies of the elite rose to their feet with their eyes rolled back into their skulls and their veins popping out all over their bodies.

"You guys, ok?" X said.

A dark shroud of energy began to be expelled around each one of them. Michael's body began to charge, its fist full of energy.

"Hey Michael, you really don't like bugs–"

Michael landed a direct punch to X's gut; X felt the full impact of the punch as he spit up blood. Bird pulled the shotgun out of the sheath on his back. Hearing the pump of the gun, X moved with a flash as Bird took aim at him and fired. With great speed, X moved to a safe distance or so he thought as he was tapped on the shoulder by Grid then punched through a building. Trying to recover, he looked at the floor; as water flooded the building X knew that Ref was behind this one.

"Good one, Ref, but I don't want to fight you guys."

The water began to form into Ref. "Too bad."

X's body, being already damp, stood in a small puddle. Ref shocked the water sending a shock through X's body. X dropped to his knees, feeling the pain. He thought to himself, "My only options are either to escape or to fight, and I can't kill my friends." X suddenly had an idea – none of these elite members could travel through portals.

"Ref, I'm not going to fight, but I need to find a way to cure you and the rest, so with that being said I need some space." Picking up his wrist to snap his fingers, X felt as pull at his arm it was Michael.

"You're not getting away." Michael threw X back outside through a wall.

Grid caught X's battered body and held him in a headlock.

Bird walked over, holding a metal baseball bat. "Maybe we don't want to be cured." He took a swing to the gut of X.

X coughed up more blood and struggled to catch his breath. "All of your abilities are great, don't get me wrong, but I'm getting pretty tired of being smacked around.

Michael landed next to Bird and spoke in a possessed voice. "If you go into your rage mode, you will kill us. Can you live with that?"

X laughed. "No I couldn't, so here's what I'm going to do." X winked his eye, and a bulletproof box was around him and Grid. "That's to stop the bullet that Bird was about to shoot."

A bullet ricocheted off the glass, hitting Michael in the shoulder. X then used Ref's ability to fill up the cube with water, and he gave Grid an ultimatum. "Either you pass out drowning or I let you out!"

Grid locked his grip tighter.

"Ok, have have it your way."

The water began to fill the cube very fast. As it passed their necks, X was relieved Grid did not call his bluff as he released his lock and tried to create an exit. X charged his fist with electricity and punched the panicking Grid. Snapping his fingers, a hole opened in the back of the cube. X kicked Grid through with the water. Snapping his fingers once more to seal the hole, X knew he had had a very small time frame to find a cure before the cube would be destroyed with him in it.

"These bugs are a like a virus, he thought out loud, "so I have to create an antivirus and enough of it to stop however many are inside of them. My antivirus must kill and extract the bugs without killing everyone in; being that the bugs are clamping down on to every organ that is needed to do anything I have to be extremely careful."

Michael and the rest of elite were attacking the cube with everything while X was in deep thought. Bird began to arm an RPG supercharged with Ref's energy to an atomic proportion.

"X, you're coming out of there or we're gonna kill ya!"

As the grenade was fired, X slowed down time and space, as his antivirus filled the cube. X then opened a portal behind Bird and the others. "This one is for you Black Jack!"

Time was back to normal the grenade landing a direct hit on the cube turning it Into dust.

"Ref, did we kill him?"

As the smoke cleared, the elite saw no remains. Ref turned to Bird. "Do you hear buzzing?"

Turning around, they only saw X surrounded by a thick cloud, his eyes glowing to activate his wind powers sending the antivirus at the elite in a huge gust of wind. The antiviral swarmed the elite, entered their bodies, and immediately began clearing the body of all infections. Once more, the elite fell to the ground rolling in pain.

Ref was the first to recover. "The bugs, the fucking bugs!"

X flew down to Ref. "Hey, hey, be easy, you're ok, I took care of them."

Grid was the next to recover. "Bugs! I fucking hate bugs!"

Ref and X laughed, Ref grabbed his shoulder. "We're cool now. I have an idea – everyone start to slap Bird when he comes to." They nodded.

Michael was the next to come to. "What happened?"

"Long story, hold on," X said.

Bird began to come to. X, Ref and Grid began to slap and smack Bird as if they were trying to swat and kill bugs. Bird began to yell, "Get 'em off me, get 'em off me!"

Ref tried to hold in his laughter. "We killed them, you're ok."

Michael shook his head in the background. "Idiots."

Waters was the last to come to. When they were all cured, Michael said, "So X, tell us."

X shrugged. "You guys got infected, tried to kill me. I kicked into high gear and made moves trying not to kill you all. The end."

Ref looking confused.

X looked at him. "Some of you displayed abilities that I did not even know you could do."

Ref in shock. "Like what?"

"You materialized into water.

At that very moment, X dropped to one knee in pain as he coughed up blood

Grid rushed over. "Now what?"

"I've obviously been infected, too; I just wasn't possessed. Hold on."

Before the elites' eyes, a massive swarm of antiviral bugs poured from their bodies into X's. Within seconds, X was back on his feet, the elite again were amazed by X's abilities.

X continued. "Ok, so if Black Jack is not in heaven or on earth, there is only one place he can be."

༃⃛ Chapter 20 ༃⃛

Stumbling into the next into the next room of the castle, Y was pretty fed up with this back-to-back fighting. "I don't know about you guys," he said, "but I need a fucking break."

Looking around the room, there was a cozy fireplace area with paintings everywhere and fine furniture. Walking up to a table, he saw a book with the title "Mein Kampf." As Y reached for the book, a voice was heard from a large chair in front of the fire: "That book is unspeakable evil. Just touching that book is bad for ones thoughts."

"Who's there?"

A tall, well-dressed man rose out if his seat to greet the three. "A popular expression on earth is that 'Money makes the world go round.' Well, that's funny; I say sin is what makes hell thrive."

With a confused look on his face Y said, "Who are you, and why should we care about your analogies and theory?"

The gentleman turned his back to Y. "It doesn't matter who I am or where I came from – or does it Y?"

"You know my name?"

"Your name is just one of many things I know about you. Another thing would be how you use to get drunk and beat and rape your wife whenever coming home from work. Or let's talk about the things you have done before the wife and kid – shall we the mercenary work, all the contracts to protect the blood diamond-mining filth killing all those innocent children!" Suddenly the gentleman began to clap. "Bravo."

"Fuck you, that's what life is all about, making it your bitch, and that's what I did and that's how I roll. So let me guess, you're here to tell me to turn back after you sent hundreds of demons after us. Fuck you, your throne, it's mine."

The gentleman stopped clapping. "Cocky child. I've been here thousands of years. You think you would be the first to challenge me? I gotta tell ya, being down here for so long, the things I have accomplished, the things I have witnessed, and the reputation I have built, every time a person sins I grow stronger, and it's a beautiful thing."

Y was not convinced by the speech and yawns.

Vimarra stepped forward. "Dark King, I have brought the spy of heaven before you, and I would like my reward."

The Dark King turns to Vimarra. "You have done well. I grant you full access to my kingdom. Live lavishly in slender, my child." Waving his hand over Vimarra, a tattoo – the mark of the beast or "666" – appeared on her neck.

Y rolled his eyes not wanting to take away Vimarra's moment, but he knew she was full of shit. "Ok so now that I am here, how about we settle this?" Taking the scythe out from behind his back, he charged it with dark energy.

The Dark King laughed. "If that's all of the power you have, I'm really disappointed." Waving his hand, the room began to transform. The temperature began to rise, as bricks began falling from the walls and the floor began to crumble underneath. Everyone began to levitate, watching as the room turning into what looked like the inside of a volcano. "Welcome to the true view of my home. Hell is supposed to be a true place of fire and brimstone, but like I said, I have been here for a while, so why not have the comforts of real–"

"Shut up. Who cares? In about 10 seconds it's going to be a sports bar and bowling alley."

The Dark King laughed again. "Ok then, I will reveal my true form." Waving his hands once more, tiny horns popped out of his skull, a serpent's tail fell from his backside, the suit on his body turned to ash, as his skin turned also the color ash, his eyes turned into the eyes of goats that glowed blue, and the weapon of choice – the trident of the Dark King – was revealed as the lava below them began to act unstable.

Y smirked. "Finally, a real fight." He transformed into his own half-demon-like state.

The Dark King without hesitation commanded his trident, raising a wave of lava then making it fall toward Y. Twirling the scythe, Y generated its power then sliced through the wave rushing for the Dark King. The Dark King met his attack with his trident, pushing Y back then raising another lava wave. Y dodged it but was blindsided by the Dark King ramming Y with his horns with a head butt. Y flew into the burning hot wall. As trying to maintain composure, the Dark King with great speed sped to his location. Grabbing his head by the hair, the Dark King slammed it continuously into the burning hot wall. Feeling the pain, Y winked, and his head was covered with a helmet.

The Dark King laughed. "That's not going to stop the pain." He continued to slam Y's head into the wall.

Y waited for the right moment when the Dark King would have a full grip of the helmet, and just as he thought the Dark King held his head against the burning hot wall and said, "You're no match, boy," the helmet against his hand sprang into action. Tiny holes opened up in the helmet, releasing tiny spiked barbs piercing the Dark King's hand.

The Dark King pulled back his hand in shock with a dozen tiny bleeding holes in his hand. Once more the Dark King laughed. "Again, great surprise but watch this." The Dark King grabbed the arm of the bleeding hand with a good grip and pulled it out of its socket still laughing. "Ready?" He tore the whole arm off his body.

Y was grossed out but kept his cool still watching, as the Dark King's blood began to pour out his wound, then some of the blood squirted on Y. Y then began to notice the missing arm formed a tiny black tail. The Dark King also began to pull on it. As he pulled it out more, it revealed a long tentacle. The blood around the tentacle began to turn green and slimy. The Dark King whipped the tentacle arm at Y, who instantly slashed it with the scythe. The Dark King smirked and pulled back the tentacle whip. Where it was cut, it turned into two tentacles that slashed at Y. Y slashed them both, the Dark King pulled them back as they turned into four and whipped them back out. Y slashed them again, turning them into eight. Not realizing that every time he cut not only did they multiply but they became faster, and with sixteen tentacles Y felt like he was just fighting the arm itself.

"I really should not fucking cut anymore," Y said, as using his speed to dodge the swinging tentacles. Y could only keep his eye on so many at once and only had two arms at that. Slapping away whichever tentacles he could, the ones that hit him were like whips cracking against him. Some of the tentacles began to wrap around his leg and threw him off balance. Another two tentacles wrapped around the scythe trying to pull it from his grip, activating Squylir to urgently protect the wielder of the scythe. Squylir flew straight toward the Dark King forming his shadow-like body into that of a giant fist and crashing into the Dark King. The Dark King, along with Y, were sent flying, smashing into the burning walls of the lair.

The scythe was glowing, as if it had shown one of its true abilities. Y was amazed. "Wow what else can this shit do?" The tentacles were wrapped tightly around his legs, though, and he could feel them starting to go numb. "Squylir, get me free!"

Squylir's body turned into a giant shadow blade cutting through the Dark King's grip.

The Dark King spit. "Now I recognize that toy – the Reaper's scythe. How unique a weapon! I bet you don't even know what it's capable of."

Y laughed. "Tell me." Squylir turning back into his normal body with a look of possession. "Nice, I'm free and can feel my leg."

The Dark King began to yell, holding his body as he began to exhaust a great amount of power. "I'll show you the true power of the king of hell!" The trident began to glow a bright red, and the tentacle arm began to braid together into one big arm. Taking grip of the trident in both arms and raising it above his head, power began to generate into the trident, as it began to charge. Pointing the tip at Y, the trident let of a huge beam of energy at Y.

Squylir jumped in the way. "Squylir, no you won't be able to survive," Y said, as grasping down firmly onto the scythe and reaching out to Squylir with the other. As the scythe's hidden power activated once more, Y unintentionally froze time and opened a portal into space. "What the fuck is this? A random piece of shit!"

Y moved Squylir out of the way, switching the Dark King into Squylir's position. The time warp ended, as the Dark King was engulfed in his own energy, and the beam passed through his body tearing it to shreds. The Dark King's body is bleeding profusely and uncontrollably.

"Looks like you beat," Y said, as the Dark King dropped to the lava below. Y snapped his fingers, creating a rope catching the Dark King's body from falling.

"You're saving me?"

Y shook his head, as he charged up the scythe with his own energy slashing right down the center of the Dark Kings body, obliterating it.

At that very moment, the room began to change back to its original state. Y held the charged scythe looking the the ashes of the Dark King then kicking them into them fireplace. "I wasn't saving you I was making sure you would not regenerate or some shit," he said.

As the ashes hit the fire, a laugh came from the flames.

⳥ⳡ Chapter 21 ⳥ⳡ

As the battle between heaven and hell began to rage, the people of earth were torn between the chaos. Humans first began to notice that no one was dying. Without an actual Reaper to guide the souls into heaven or hell, earth became its own place of chaos. The angel army was trying its best to keep the chaos to a minimum; even without the Reaper, fallen angels and demons had no new vessels to inhabit, so they would be forced to stay in the decaying vessel.

It seemed like the elite had swept over the whole planet by and had even combed heaven with a fine tooth comb, but Black Jack was nowhere to be found. Then Michael had took notice to Gabriel and his strange activity even more. It had seemed as though Gabriel's wings were beginning to turn gray, and his facial expression was always the same; his pupils became enlarged, and the possessed state became worse.

"Will someone tell me what's wrong with messenger boy? Michael said. "Why is he acting so strange?" Putting his hand near Gabriel's face, Gabriel tried to bite his hand. "What the hell?"

Gabriel looked at Michael. "The new wielder of the scythe is coming for you all, and a new revolution will begin."

Looking perplexed, Michael called X over. "X, if what Gabriel is saying is true, we might have a problem on our hands."

X turned to the possessed Gabriel. "Who is this wielder of the scythe? What is this revolutionary move he is going to make?"

Gabriel began to rock back and forth, as laughing.

X slapped him. "Seriously, knock it off and tell us the outcome."

"The outcome could be either side. Both of you have great unimaginable power; you have slain so many demons and fight alongside

Michael, the strongest of the angels, but can you take out the man who just defeated the Dark King?"

X looked at Michael. "The Dark King? Who is the Dark King?"

Bird chimed in. "The devil, the antichrist, Satan, whatever name you want to call him, he's evil."

X looked back at Gabriel. "This guy took out the devil, huh? That's insane. So you think I can take him?"

"You both share similar power; however, fighting him will either be the apocalypse or the salvation of many world's."

X grabbed Gabriel by the arm. "What do you mean by apocalypse?"

Gabriel, exhausted from his possessed state, passed out.

Michael turned to X and then looked at the rest of the elite. "If we are to stop what's coming, we need to prepare. From what things sound like, we could have a bad situation on our hands, soldiers, so everyone let's get ready for the fight of the eternity. As soon as this asshole wakes up, we're going to cut him loose. Someone must volunteer to trail him to get us some Intel on this dark scythe lunatic."

Bird nodded.

"Take Grid with you just in case shit gets heavy. The rest of us will gather our remaining troops and meet back on earth."

⳾Ɛ⳾ Chapter 22 ⳾Ɛ⳾

Ever since the fall of the Dark King, Y had been getting use to his new home. "How did this guy live here? This place sucks."

Vimarra laughed. "Well, it was never meant to be a pleasant place."

Y smiled. "Oh yeah? Watch this." He closed his eyes and focused taking a deep breath.

Vimarra watched closely. "Well?"

Y snapped his fingers. The kingdom was transformed into a giant man cave with giant TVs, bars, comfortable furniture, and hot tubs. "Yeah that's more like it."

Vimarra shook her head. "What a pig."

Y yawned, as he sank into a chair. "Shut up," he said, and snapped his fingers once more. Vimarra's outfit changed into a sexy ensemble of black lingerie, and her chest enlarged, almost exploding out of the bra

Disgusted but turned on at the same time, Vimarra said, "Change them back please. Oh, and as the new King, you should have a queen."

Y interrupted. "Yeah yeah, fine."

A crown appeared above Vimarra's horns. "As hell's new king, don't you think you should address the demon army?"

Y looking at Vimarra. "Ok fine. How do we go about that?"

"Let's go to Blood Lake now."

Y rose to his feet. "Ok let's go." Tapping the bottom of the scythe on the ground, a portal opened to Blood Lake. Again Y was mystified. "I really need to learn how to use this thing."

Upon arrival, Blood Lake was empty.

Y looked at Vimarra. "Where is my army?"

Vimarra looking around. "There should be a gong somewhere around here." Spotting it, she pointed.

Y walked over to it. The gong was the size of a pickup truck. Picking up the massive mallet, Y smacked the gong. As it sounded, the ground began to shake and Blood Lake began to boil. Thousands of demons began to rise out of the soil and hundreds began to fill the air over the lake. The demons were confused as they looked at Y standing next to the gong.

One demon pointed at Y. "Who the fuck are you?"

Another demon yelled, "Weren't we supposed to kill that asshole?"

Y began to laugh. Snapping his fingers, a stage with a podium rose from under his feet.

The demons were astonished. "How the fuck did you do that?" one shouted.

Another demon yelled out, "Cheap magic trick!"

Y walked to the podium and grabbed the microphone. "It looks like you all have many questions – many great questions – but the main question I liked was 'Who the fuck are?' That was my favorite one. So who am I? I am your new ruler. The Dark King is dead."

The crowd began to laugh in a uproar.

Y began to laugh, too. "Yeah, this is funny, very funny, but ask yourselves, why am I here and he is not?"

The uproar ended, and one demon spoke. "He's got a point – but even if he is dead, why should we care?"

"Because hell should be fun, not a place of misery right?"

The demons looked confused.

"Imagine this – you get to chill every day and do the fun shit you liked to do when you were alive." Y pointed to a random demon. "You over there, what was fun to you?"

The demon replied, "It was fun to murder people when I was human."

"The point being that it was fun, so no more torture under my rule and no more misery. As a matter of fact, do whatever ya want, but don't bother me 'cause I'll kill ya."

The demons talked among each other then one spoke to Y. "What if we want to go to the world of the living?"

"Hey, do as you please, but remember this – you all fight for me."

The demons all agreed that Y was the new king of hell. Y raised his scythe, and the demons all raised their weapons. As the scythe opened a portal back into the kingdom, Y thought to himself, "Perfect timing, scythe."

ᏮᏤᎷᏤᎷ Chapter 23 ᏮᏤᎷᏤᎷ

A possessed Gabriel awakened and noticed he was not in the the straightjacket any more. He pulled his dagger from his bag and looking around to defend himself in case any angels were to come near. The coast was clear. Locking the dagger closely in his palms, he jabbed the dagger before him and as turning it like a key, a portal began to open into hell. He walked through.

Grid and Bird followed.

Gabriel flew through hell directly to where the scythe was guiding him, as he was a slave to its power. He was connected to its aura like a heat-seeking missile. Grid and Bird following closely, as Gabriel flew deeper into the depths of hell, while traveling eyes began to take notice As two demon guards rushed to Gabriel, Grid was about to help when Bird grabbed him by the shoulder. Staying quiet, Bird pointed to Gabriel, who was fighting off the guards killing them flawlessly and continuing on his way. Grid was amazed by Gabriel's skills, and Bird looked confused.

Nearing the basement, Grid and Bird could see that the demons looked like they were having one big party. Bird looked even more confused, and Grid shook his head, as Gabriel flew down into the basement. Grid could see that it was even more heavily guarded, but every guard that tried to stop Gabriel was with little effort. Gabriel barged into the the room where Y and Vimarra sat upon their throne.

Y was pissed off. "Ok what, who the fuck are you?"

Gabriel was silent. "You are the new wielder of the scythe?"

"So what if I am?"

Gripping the scythe handle, Gabriel dropped to one knee. "I am your humble assistant, Gabriel."

Squylir appeared out of the shadows. "It's true – our souls are attached to the scythe to protect who ever wields it."

Y rose from his throne and looking over Gabriel. "You're an angel?"

"Yes, the Reaper appointed myself and Squylir as his assistants to help guide the entity that resides in you to a new vessel after the body was decomposed. Usually the minute the body stops beating, we take the entity from the body, but this time the entity has actively kept the body from decomposition after death. It seems to have an attachment to your soul."

Y clapped. "This is crazy, but you know what? You can start your new job for me by killing those two other angels that are hiding over there."

Gabriel turning around to see Grid and Bird came out of hiding and walking toward him.

"Gabriel, tell your friend to tell us what happened to our friend."

Gabriel removed the dagger from his bag. Y laughed and snapped his fingers. Suddenly Gabriel's clothes turned into a white suit with black wings, and the dagger turned into a katanna with a black blade. Gabriel charged at Bird, who pulled a large Bowie knife from his chest piece to meet the blade of Gabriel. Squylir slithered over to wrap around Grid; as soon as Grid noticed Squylir below him, he punched the ground below him, causing the floor to quake. Bird continues to block Gabriel's continuous attacks.

With his free arm, Bird pulled a Desert Eagle from his holster. "Gabriel, I'm giving you a last chance to tell us where Black Jack is."

Gabriel slashed at Bird, who dodged it by ducking low then gave Gabriel an uppercut, sending him flying toward the ceiling. Squylir slithered to the ceiling to save his comrade by cushioning the impact. Gabriel spread his wings, as Squylir wrapped around his arm, creating a weapon that seemed to be charging up dark energy and firing at Bird and Grid

Bird shot charged bullets back at Gabriel while dodging, and Grid zipped around the bullets with ease, as his speed allowed him to. Mainly paying attention to Bird, Gabriel allowed Grid to tackle him from behind, forcing him to drop the katanna.

Bird locked the Desert Eagle's sight on Gabriel. "Grid, let go."

Grid kicked off of Gabriel, and Bird let off the round pinpointed for Gabriel's head. *Tap tap.* Time froze, as the bullet was in midflight and Grid in mid acrobatics. *Tap tap,* time continued.

Y held the bullet in one hand then caught Gabriel with the arm holding the scythe. "You angels are strong, I'll give you that, but against me let's see how you do."

Bird replied, "Bring it."

Y took a deep breath, and fire began to shoot from his mouth. Bird and Grid dodged. Bird began to shoot, but Y smacked all of of the bullets down with the scythe and began to charge it's energy. Grid, using his speed, grabbed the scythe. Y grabbed Grid by the neck and threw him into Bird. With the scythe fully charged, Y unleashed the energy. Bird and Grid braced themselves for impact.

Suddenly, a portal opened, shooting a beam of light and negating the dark energy wave. X and Ref appear out of the beam, grabbed Grid and Bird, and pulled them into the portal. Y's eyes met with X's on the way into the portal, causing a chain reaction followed by a huge explosion.

Y felt the kingdom around him begin to crumble. Tapping the scythe to the floor once more, he froze time, grabbed his queen and Gabriel, and pulling them to the exit of the kingdom. Once outside of the castle, Y unfroze time.

The castle entrance caved in. Y was not mad but excited, though, and exclaimed, "Who the fuck was that?"

𐦂𐦂𐦂 Chapter 24 𐦂𐦂𐦂

X and the rest returned to heaven through the portal. Bird began to feel his hands around his body. "I'm alive, sweet."

Grid also was surprised. "That dude was crazy down there, not to mention Gabriel. Did you see the cannon on his arm? He had a cannon on his arm!"

Michael and Waters soon appeared. "Ok guys, give me the info," Michael said.

Bird started. "Gabriel is psycho, and this Y guy is really psycho."

Grid chimed in. "Whoever has the scythe controls Gabriel and some shadow thing."

Michael was in deep thought. "Gabriel is the assistant to the Reaper, so that means that this Y guy killed the Dark King and the reaper?"

Bird shrugged. "I guess so."

"That would explain why no one is dying."

X interrupted. "We have to restore the order of things, don't we? There's something I must mention – on the way out of the portal our eyes locked. At the very moment of exiting, there was an explosion."

"What kind of explosion? Did he try to attack?"

"I don't know."

"Ok, so here's the plan. The troops are ready; it looks like we need to get that scythe away from the Y guy. It's probably going to take me and X to get this job done."

Bird stepped in. "No, you can't. You must remain here in heaven and protect our kind."

Michael smiled. "Yeah, but they have the power to come up here anyway."

Ref stepped forward. "That's what you have us for — we should demand that we meet. I'm going to the earth realm to finish this. Bring the army, everyone goes and hit 'em with everything we got. It's obvious they won't hold back. Neither will we!"

X grabbed Ref by the shoulder. "We got this, let's go." Then X remembered Gabriel's warning about an apocalypse. "Guys, let's try to wait a couple of days. There is something I need to do."

Michael nodded. "Ok. In the meantime, everyone get back to the barracks and train 'til we are ready!"

❧❦☙ Chapter 25 ❧❦☙

Y did not rebuild the kingdom. Instead, he chose to be around Blood Lake pondering the abilities of this scythe that was in his possession. "How do you work?" He looked at Gabriel. "How does this thing work?"

"The scythe can control time and space, open portals between heaven and hell and also into other dimensions."

"Other dimensions?"

"Yes, the domain of the Reaper does not exist in realms like hell or heaven."

"How would one open a portal dimension?"

Gabriel was silent for a moment. "I'm sorry, I do not know. I have never used the scythe before."

Finding his assistant to be quite useless, Y began to experiment. "Maybe if you hold it a certain way…Tapping the bottom froze time, the one arm point opens a portal…let's try the one arm point hand wave!"

Nothing happened. In frustration, Y the scythe still and throwing his arm up then down with his palm open, opened a small vortex. Looking into the eye of it, Y smirked.

His success was interrupted when a random demon came up and waited to be addressed.

Y turning around slightly annoyed. "Yes?"

"While I was terrorizing the humans, your lordship, I was forced back into hell by an angel, who first shocked me then burned me then he slammed me into a–"

"Get to the point, dude. Clearly you got your ass kicked."

The angel sent me back with a message. It said to meet them 'on the earth realm, bitch.'"

Y starting to laugh. "Wait they really said 'bitch?'"

"No, I threw that last part in cause you cut me off in mid story"

Y laughed some more. "I like you, come over here."

The demon walked up, then Y snapped his fingers turning his fist into steel, punched the demon's mouth through his teeth, and ripped his tongue out.

As the demon dropped to the ground writhing in pain, Y stood over him. "I know this is hell, but you still will respect the king." He tossed the demon's bloody tongue back at him then looked at Gabriel. "Prepare my army."

Gabriel nodded, pointed out the demon Y just injured was one of his generals, then continued to the barracks.

Vimarra was lying down in a beach chair wearing a bathing suit. Y looked at her. "Vimarra, aren't you going to prepare for battle?"

Vimarra shook her head. "What for? I have already achieved the goal I was trying to reach. I'm queen of hell. How about this – I'll hold down the fort while you boys hash it out?"

Y smirked. "Like we needed you anyway."

"By the way, if you want a stronger army, you need to make sacrifices into Blood Lake.

"Let's start by throwing you in."

Vimarra smirked. "Don't even think about it."

Y turned his back then transformed his body into his demon form and flew away to meet Gabriel and the troops. Upon arrival, Y was pleased to see such a vast number of soldiers at his disposal. "Ok assholes, line up!" he shouted.

The demons organized themselves.

"Ok, march into Blood Lake."

Gabriel was confused. "Your Lordship, your numbers will decrease if–"

Y interrupted, "But the results will will be better. You fought those angels and you know how strong they were!"

Millions of demons marched into Blood Lake, which began to overflow from the capacity, as a vast array of colors shot out of the lake. Over it, six beings hovered in midair and looked toward Y.

He flew to them. "This is my ultimate army?"

The six were demons with bodies shaped like humans ranging in size and all wearing silver and black armor with a design that looked like faded blood splatter. They wore masks of different varieties to tell each other apart, and they carried a variety of weapons.

Y was excited. "I think I can work with this." Opening a portal to earth, the six demons, including Gabriel, followed Y.

❧❦❧ Chapter 26 ❧❦❧

An alarm in heaven began to sound. Michael looking at his group of elite and was proud. "My soldiers, the time has come. Let's bring back the balance."

Looking at X to open the portal into earth, h did so. Michael entered first, followed by the elite and X. As soon as they all appeared in the earth realm, the air suddenly became a mass of thunderclouds. A football field's length away, the ground began to quake, the wind began to pick up into a hurricane. The two small armies stared at each other waiting for the first sign of movement.

Michael was the first to speak. "I want to send all of you back to hell."

Y laughed. "I don't know who you are, but it seems like you're in a hurry to die here today."

"Hand over the scythe, and you all can return home in one piece."

Y smirked. "I earned this trophy and this title. You want it, then take it from me – simple as that!" Pointing the scythe at the elite, the six demons including Gabriel began to fly down the battlefield.

Michael began to levitate and drew his sword. "Fuck 'em up!"

The elite launched for the six demons and Gabriel. Michael stayed behind, watching Y to see if he would make a move. All of a sudden, he decided to go for Y.

Y was delighted with the challenge, and spreading his wings flew higher for more space. Michael gave chase.

Ref meeting with the Gabriel-Squylir combination, "Gabriel, what happened to you? Snap out of it."

As Squylir turned into a whip, Gabriel replied, "My loyalty does not belong to good or evil; it belongs to the scythe." Lashing the whip out to Ref's arm, he and pulling Ref in to cut him with the katana. Ref turned his arm into stone as the blade bounced off with harsh recoil. He then yanked the whip toward himself, punching Gabriel with the stone fist.

Meanwhile, Bird coming face to face with one of the six. Bird was ready for anything, but the demon just stood still there in front of him. "Well then, what do you do?"

The demon lowered itself to the ground and calmly planted his hands against the soil. Suddenly headstones began to pop out of the ground. The demon picked up of of the large headstones and was about to swing it at Bird. Bird pulled for his shotgun but was distracted feeling a slight pull at his ankle. It was a hand. Catching Bird off guard, the demon slammed the headstone into him sending Bird flying through other graves.

As Bird came to on top of a pile of rubble, he wiped some blood from his mouth. "That was cheap."

Suddenly, right in front of Bird more hands began to come out of the ground attached to rotting and decaying bodies. They were the undead.

Bird could not believe his eyes. He pulled out two pistols. "Ok, let's play." He began to shoot at everything in sight.

Meanwhile, X was up against two demons when he noticed Michael going after Y. As one of the demons rushed, X calmly dodged its attack then grabbing it by the arm flung it back into the other demon. One demon pulled out a doll while the other started to attack X, wildly throwing punches and kicks that X had no problem dodging. The demon holding the doll stretched out the limbs, and X's opponent became taller and was still punching and kicking at X with everything it had. X was starting to be slightly amused by the demon; he even met one of the punches with with a block then returned a punch knocking the demon back. Stumbling over the other, X took the doll from the other demon.

"This is cool," X said, "let me borrow it; I'll show you how to make a cool creature."

X molded the arms of the doll into four then made the arms pointy like blades. The demon began to transform. X tossed the doll back to the other demon. "That's cool." As the four-armed sword-hand demon came after him, X snapped his fingers creating two swords in each hand to block the onslaught of attacks from the demon, who sent after barrage of attacks his way. The demon holding the doll twisted the torso around making the other demon spin rapidly. X was amazed. "Now that's cool!" he said then looked up into the clouds wondering how Michael was doing.

Grid was faced by the largest of the demons, which was fine with Grid because he liked to test his might and speed. The demon walked up to Grid, who wasn't that much smaller than himself. The demon threw a punch at Grid, hitting him in the face. Grid flew back sliding on his back then tucking into into a roll and sliding on one knee, spitting out a bit of blood. He yelled, "Ok my turn," and with a burst of speed and strength Grid tackled the demon through a building and inside another. The demon grabbed Grid by his left wing to pull him off and flung him through another wall. While trying to stand to his knees, the demon was slow and bulky, so by the time he stood up the speedy Grid was already back in his face delivering smooth and heavy punches, first one to his gut then another to his face. The demon caught his next punch slamming his fist into the wall to unball his fist then kicked Grid back outside, sliding into a horde of zombies that Bird was battling.

"Bird, what the fuck is this?"

"Dog I don't know I got hit with a graveI'm here."

Grid requested a switch. "What do you got?"

"Medium-sized weird grave, dude. You?"

"Big, fat, slow asshole coming this way."

Bird had a quick split decision. "How about this – we work together?" He took out a flash grenade tossing it toward the big fat demon. As soon as the flash went off, they both went for the other, Bird taking out a shotgun charged with electricity clearing the way of the zombies when he noticed another tombstone flying through the crowd right at him. He blasted right through it, then another grave flew right at Grid, who caught it.

Throwing the grave back where it came from, Grid being frustrated from the zombies and slammed his fist against the ground, causing a tremor. All the zombies fell to the ground. Only the demon, Grid and Bird were on their feet. Grid zipped across to the demon, who was holding a headstone. Grid grabbed it from him and smacked the demon in the back of the head, sending it flying into Bird.

Bird caught the demon by the neck. "Payback bitch." He cocked his head back then delivering a head butt. The demon's eyes rolled back into its skull. Bird stuffed a grenade into its mouth then quickly kicked the demon toward the fatter demon. Bird's demon exploded, but the explosion did nothing to injure the fat demon. The fat demon merely shook it off he continued to make his way to Bird and Grid.

༕✂༏༕ Chapter 27 ༕✂༏༕

Ref continued his battle with Gabriel. Gabriel had always wanted to prove he was a worthy opponent, but the other angels always thought of him as being a worthless grunt with the powers of darkness his abilities were increased along with Squylir he could prove himself although Ref was not going down easy.

"Gabriel, last chance – don't make me finish you and the other assistant if there will ever be a new Reaper they might need you."

"You elite members think you're hot shit. I'll start with you and then finish the rest."

Ref stayed quiet then began to charge his fist with lightning. "If you think you're going to take out the elite starting with me, you're mistaken."

Gabriel changed Squylir into a more aggressive cannon with a large barrel, and began to fire a huge dark energy beam at Ref. Ref took to the sky flying through the clouds while dodging the beams. Gabriel chased Ref through the clouds continuously shooting.

Thunder began to light up the sky. One flash of lightning blinded Gabriel, causing him to lose sight of Ref. "You think I don't know that's you manipulating the weather?" Gabriel yelled out of frustration, as he began to randomly shoot the beam into the clouds while rain beads fell upon his face. "Show yourself, coward!"

Ref's body began to slowly materialize itself behind Gabriel. Gabriel then noticed a massive charge of electricity behind him, then Ref palmed Gabriel's face, sending a shock through Gabriel's body. The toasted Gabriel began to fall to the ground. Ref following close by. As soon as Gabriel's body hit the ground, Ref landed next to it. The mud around Gabriel's body began to swallow him, leaving only his head visible. Gabriel could feel his body being constricted by the mud.

"You bastard!" he shouted.

"Keep quiet. We'll be back for you soon when this is all over" Ref then flew over to meet Bird, suddenly being knocked into by Waters.

Waters trying to collect himself. "Are they still on me?"

Ref looking over his shoulder. "I don't see anything – where is the demon?"

Waters was trying to collect himself but as soon as he tried to locate the demon, his head began to hurt.

"Waters, what's going on?" Suddenly Ref was hit with a large psychic blast hurtling him into the side of a building. Ref looked around, could not see where the blast came from. Then all of a sudden he felt his body being pulled again; whoever was doing the pulling revealed themselves a large muscular demon holding the side of its head. "So it's you! What have you done to Waters? No matter, you'll fix 'em in a couple seconds."

The demon smirked as a car came flying at Ref and crashed into him and Waters. Waters spit blood on the hood of the car.

"Waters, snap out of it and heal us real quick," Ref said.

Waters was able to heal them. Ref told Waters to hold on as a gust of wind slowed the car down from smacking into a wall, then the gust became stronger, pushing the car back toward the demon. The demon, seeing the car flying his way, tried to push It back harder with his mind. He managed to make the car slow down a bit until Ref noticed as his eyes turned gray and red flying around the car while spinning turning it into a horizontal tornado as the car smacked into the demon. Ref turned the tornado into fire, causing the car to explode and the demon with it.

Ref regrouped with Waters. "Let's get to Bird."

Flying over the battlefield, Ref could not see Michael. He could see X, though, and figured X could handle the two he was fighting. Then he saw the fat demon battling Bird and Grid. "Whoa!"

Landing next to Bird, he said, "Yo Bird, that looks like one fat ugly."

"No time to talk; this mother fucker is eating everything I throw at him – all the bullets, grenades –even Grid can't get get a good hit on him."

Ref was stunned. "Waters, heal them while I find a weakness." Bird and Grid huddled around Waters for a couple of seconds, as Ref flew around then came back. "My guess is we have to attack from the inside.

Keep feeding it energy until it gets big enough to eat one of us. Plant a charge then get out."

Bird laughed. "That's stupid. I'm not going in there!"

"Why not?"

Grid interrupted. "Can we figure out what we're going to do, 'cause he's attacking?"

A massive hand came crashing down over them, but Grid caught it. "Guys, move!"

Bird, Ref and Waters scrambled. Then Bird yelled at Ref, "Give me the energy!"

"I thought you weren't going in?"

"I'm not watching this."

Bird flew over the demon's head and out a revolver. Ref recognized the gun.

"Ok let's do this!" Bird shot the first round.

Ref charged it with lightning. The round hit the demon's eye, creating an opening, then Bird fired the second round. Ref charged it with fire as it hit the second eye. The third shot went off. Ref covered the shot in water then blasted it with cold air, making a larger ice bullet, as it smashed in between the demon's eyes taking out three plastics of C-4. Bird tossed them to Ref; he filled them each with elemental energy and dropped them into each hole. The demon writhed in pain as waving its arms uncontrollably, trying trying to smash whatever it could hit.

Ref yelled, "Bird now!"

Bird flew in the opposite direction of Ref and fired three bullets that upon impact caused the charge to explode. As Bird, Grid, Ref and Waters flew for cover, the massive explosion sent fat zombie pieces flying everywhere. Bird in celebration threw a fist to Ref, as Ref smashed his against Bird's. "We always practiced that never thought we would get to use it!"

Bird laughed. "I call that the six-round pound."

Ref laughed. "What! That's funny as hell."

𝔢𝔤𝔠𝔧𝔢 Chapter 28 𝔢𝔤𝔠𝔧𝔢

X looked down and seeing the elite was all in top shape knew that this was his chance. Looking at the demon controlling the other one, X snapped his fingers, turning one of the swords into a pistol. He shot the doll out of the demon's hands then with great speed collected the doll, smashed it into a ball and shot it with a bullet charged with his own angelic energy. Both demons stopped in their tracks looking confused. X smirked and snapping his fingers turned the pistol back into a sword then charged them with energy, slashing through both demons.

"Sorry, I can't play anymore," X said then launched toward the clouds at neck-snapping speed.

X saw a fireball hurting toward the ground, but he felt that energy that passed him it was not a fireball but Michael. Michael's body hit the ground creating a crater, and X rushed down arriving first to a bloody and battered Michael, whose armor was cracked and his wings burned.

"Michael, hey Michael, tell me you're ok."

As the other elite rushed over to the scene, Ref said, "Is he ok?"

X with his head down closed Michael's eyelids then looked into the clouds knowing that, that lunatic was looking right at him.

Ref grabbed X's shoulder. "He's not dead, you know. Waters will take care of him; in the meantime, go finish this."

Prying Michael's sword from its sheath. The sword and its aura changed, fusing with X's power and armor. Feeling the support of his team, X launched into the clouds at full speed.

❧❦☙❧ Chapter 29 ❧❦☙❧

High above earth, almost into space, X could feel the gaze of the cold-blooded killer upon him. X's own thoughts started to get on his nerve – *What if I don't defeat him, what kind of place would the world be or the universe for that matter, would everything cease to exist?*

Y stood in the distance. "You and I aren't so different, you know."

X turned around to meet Y. The air felt very dense and heavy. "We are alike, as we have the same power, but that doesn't make us the same person." X could see the scythe on Y's back.

"You and me, X, we are gods. We can change the fate of this entire universe; it is at our mercy. Can't you see that?"

X frowned. "I'm not blind to it, but the best thing to do is to leave this place just the way it was created."

"The way it was created by the entities inside of us on accident! These powers given to me and you is fate. We are kings, and the rest are just ants! I'm asking you to join me in ruling supreme."

X laughed. "Yeah, we probably would have been good friends, but I'm not joining you. I'm not power hungry like you. And that scythe on your back is going back to its rightful owner." He pulled Michael's sword from his sheath.

Y pulled the scythe from his back. "So be it. Perish like the rest of them. That sword looks familiar. Oh yeah, I just kicked that guy's ass!"

X charged at Y with full speed. As coming within feet of Y, the latter caused an explosion strong enough to destroy half of the state of California. Even though the explosion was in the sky, the damage on the ground was extensive, causing the ground to split open exposing layers of sediment, and new mantle plumes to form as lava began to flow violently from long sleeping volcanoes. Neither X nor Y were affected from the blast, though, as they stood with their weapons at ready.

"You know as well as I do that we cannot fight here," X said.

"Duh! Not gonna destroy my kingdoms!"

X wiped his fingers along the blade while Y ran his down the scythe's blade, as they both opened a wormhole to another dimension. As the other end of the wormhole spit them out, they landed in a desolate realm of nothing but blue sand and yellow sky. Landing in a place that literally did not exist made X a lot more at ease.

Y looking around for creatures just in case. "Well, isn't this a cluster fuck?"

X was amazed but then jumped on guard, not losing focus. Putting his hand into the blue sand, he made it spike up at Y. Y dodged the spike and shot a red beam of light from his horns at X, who deflected it off the sword then came charging at Y with full speed. Y met his blade with the scythe causing yet another explosive chain reaction sending most of the blue sand into the yellow sky. As the dust rained green, X pushed Y back charging his fist with electricity and reached for Y's face. Y dodged it, sweeping the scythe around to catch X in his back. X, using his speed teleporting to escape, appeared above Y and slashed the sword downward. Y, just barely noticing, defended himself with the scythe, pushing X back. Y snapped his fingers and laser cannons pushed out of the ground and began to shoot at X. Y was content with his move and watched X scramble to dodge the blast. X snapped his fingers, sheathing Michael's sword. As two pistols appeared in his hands, he began to take out the cannons with explosive rounds.

Y thought to himself, "Damn this guy is pretty good."

X took out the last cannon then began firing at Y. Y took flight pulling aerial spins and twists to avoid the bullets then opening another wormhole to evade X. The speedy X followed closely, watchful for Y's tricks as flying through it to a new dimension.

Y did not know what to expect, either. Exiting the wormhole, he noticed an extreme heat, as if they were fighting inside of the sun. Y looking around noticing that they were indeed inside a spire of some sort of fire. Y switched to his demon form so he could withstand the heat but was tackled by an X, whose body was engulfed in flames.

Thanks to Ref's training, X could withstand the heat. He held onto Y's midsection trying to body slam him. Y countered by placing

X in a headlock then tried to slam his head into the wall of the sphere, but when he put his head, they both fell into an sphere made of water. Thinking they would instantly fall through this one, X held the sword firmly and blinked, turning the sphere to ice.

Y was not prepared to fight in ice. "What the fuck kind of dimension is this is?" Before X could unleash another attack, Y opened another wormhole below his feet sinking in.

X was tired of Y's evasion. 'Seriously, dude, just pick one to die in already." X began to think to himself that the only way to win was to get the scythe away from Y, disabling his ability to jump through any dimension or portals.

The next dimension was complete nothingness – no gravity, no light, no dark, a completely clean slate universe. X saw this and then saw Y with his back turned to him. "Looks like a quick way to lose this fight, turning your back to me," X said.

"This is what the world would be if I destroyed it along with the universe, and seeing the other dimensions I could rule it all!"

"Stop this game! What the fuck – no one will bow down to a clown like you. If you want to rule this nothingness, by all means you can stay here!" X let out a blood-curdling yell as Michael's sword began to illuminate the realm. The sword began to react to the entity inside of X's body, as a wild aura shrouded his body and his eyes glowed.

Y smirked. "You think I don't know how to do that, too?" Holding the scythe, a wide, dark and vast amount of power spread over his body, as the scythe charged its energy to the max, sending a wave of power from from the scythe unlike he had ever unleashed before. The power turned into a giant Reaper coming for X.

X did not fear but embraced the pain. As it coursed through his body, X dropped to one knee feeling the poison and the burn of the dark entity's power. Lifting his head, X laughed. "That was nice, but something is off."

Y's jaw was dropped. "You shouldn't have survived that."

"Shut up for once. All I can tell you is that what I am about to do is really going to hurt." X charged Michael's sword with the faith that he started his journey with then let go a blinding light.

Y hissed as X held the sword firmly in one hand raising his arm with the other. Then nothing happened.

"Your power is more of a dud than mine," Y said.

X flashed past Y at the speed of light and grabbed the scythe. At the moment of contact, he saw who the scythe needed to go to.

Y was furious. "How the hell did you do that?"

"That light show was just a distraction so I could get the scythe from you – or was it?" Snapping his fingers, a beam of light engulfed Y's body.

Looking into the light, Y could see the energy coming at him in the form of Michael. The power crashed through Y's body knocking the entity out the back of it. With a gaping hole in back of his body, Y turned to X. "We will will meet again." The body fell motionless then it and the entity floated into the nothingness.

❧❧ Chapter 30 ❧❧

X held the scythe and all its power. He knew the exact location of where he should go first and opened a wormhole.

As he reached the other side, a person was sitting at the entrance being blinded by X's aura. "Who are you?" the man said.

"Black Jack, it's me, X."

Black Jack was in shock to see a familiar face. "Where am I? I've been trapped here for what feels like an eternity."

"Not anymore. In fact, you're about to be able to walk anywhere you want." X presented Black Jack the scythe.

"What's that?"

X laughed. "Believe it or not, this belongs to you."

Black Jack placed his hands on the scythe, and instantly the power of the scythe was purified as its appearance began to transform with its staff turning white and gold and the blade turning into gold and white metal. Then Black Jack's wings tucked around his armor and over his head, creating a pure white shroud. His armor also dispersed, fading into a shroud of pure energy.

"You have a lot of work to do sorry it had to be this way," X said.

Jack the Reaper looked at X through a shroud. "Let's go." The Reaper opened a portal to earth and immediately freed Gabriel by placing his palm upon his forehead, undoing the evil trance he was in.

"The Reaper!" Gabriel exclaimed.

The Reaper replied, "We have work to do. Where is the other?"

Squylir came out of hiding. "Sir?"

The Reaper pointed to heaven. "You two get to work." Gabriel and Squylir immediately flew off to gather the souls of demons and angels.

Then the Reaper opened portals into hell and heaven, which sucked the souls inside. Finally, he opened a wormhole back to his domain. He waved to the elite as he passed through.

Looking at the destruction, X lowered his head "I gotta fix this, but first let's go back to heaven." Opening a portal to heaven, the elite flew in. Before the portal closed, X turned and snapping his fingers restored the earth to its original state before the war.

ཉ༽ཅ༽ཉ Chapter 31 ཉ༽ཅ༽ཉ

Y's body floated next to the aura of the evil entity. The entity floated back closely to the body as it nuzzled its way back into the body, it began to repair the damage, but feeling the warmth of the corpse the entity could feel that Y's soul was not alone.

"With the three of us, we can rule over all."

Y's eyes turned into trigrams.

THE END

❧❧ About the Author ❧❧

My name is Carlton Page. I am a multimedia major, and my passion has always been to tell people stories that I feel would be epic. I grew up watching a lot of cartoon and anime, and I read lots of comic books, so I wanted to share my views on life and the way I see it.